THE LONESOME TRAIN

Travels Through an Arkansas Childhood

Joyce Peden

ISBN: 1539122212
ISBN 13: 9781539122210
Library of Congress Control Number: 2016916292
CreateSpace Independent Publishing Platform
North Charleston, South Carolina

CONTENTS

Dedicated to my Family, my Saints and my Besties

PROLOGUE

The first years of the twentieth century were known as the Progressive Era in America. People opened up their minds and spilled out new inventions such as electricity and automobiles as well as the realization that germs cause illness.

The real Ella upon whom this novel is based, grew up in rural Arkansas during this period. She saw the advent of the Model T and the Wright brothers' accomplishment of turning a bicycle into a flying machine. She heard music being played on a Victrola and listened to stories of World War I being fought in France with modern tanks and other killing tools. She lived through the Spanish flu which killed millions.

Ella carried a song with her until her last days at age ninety three and never dwelled on the unimaginable hardships she had endured. This novel memorializes some of her recollections.

CHAPTER 1
PINE BLUFF, ARKANSAS 1918

Who would have thought that five thousand people could squeeze into the streets of modest little Pine Bluff, Arkansas, to see a parade? It did happen on Armistice Day, November 11, 1918. This was to honor our local doughboys who had come home from World War I and all the soldiers who hadn't made it back from the western front in France. Everyone bumped into each other trying to elbow into the front row to view the procession. In the air were smells of popcorn from the food stands, the scent of pine trees, and Daddy's Prince Albert pipe smoke floating skyward.

When the local Woodmen of the World band marched by, the crowd went crazy stomping and clapping and shouting. Behind the band was a float with a man on it dressed as Uncle Sam. A sign on the platform read, "The Kaiser Is Gone - Uncle Sam Lives On."

As our local heroes marched behind the platform, I saw my own brother, Mack, marching in short, choppy steps in a row of perfect formation. He moved automatically like a wooden toy soldier being blown along by the wind.

Daddy stood between my sister, Nola, and me, watching with pride, grasping our hands, a mist in his eyes. I excitedly waved and yelled, "McKinley!" but he looked straight ahead with eyes dead of expression. Daddy said Mack seemed to have left part of himself, maybe even his soul, in the war. I didn't understand grief, but life had introduced it to me anyway, and I was only thirteen years old.

The band played "Over There," and the crowd picked up the tempo and sang along "Over there, over there," clapping happily with earsplitting little yells in between words.

Dewey, my other brother, who had never met a stranger, worked the crowd from across the street. He removed his hat and gave a quick salute to Mack as he passed.

A young boy stood beside Dewey who was looking toward me with a scowl and angry brown eyes. He brushed back a swatch of thick auburn hair from his forehead and whispered something to the crippled man beside him on crutches. The man put a hand over his eyes to shield the sun and looked carefully at Daddy, then Nola, then me.

Though I remembered both the man and boy from somewhere, I couldn't put names to them. I nudged Daddy and pointed to the pair, but they vanished in the throng of five thousand. Nola interrupted my thoughts as I tried to place them.

"Come on, Sister," she said. "Let's go get some lemonade."

We got in line at the lemonade stand where the Rotary Club wives were squeezing lemons and chipping ice from big chunks. Hicks Icehouse pulled up in a wagon to deliver more blocks.

"It's about time you got here!" said Mrs. Harlen, one of the workers in the booth.

She sounded rude, but it didn't surprise me. Everyone in town knew Mrs. Harlen was low on patience.

"Two lemonades," I said to another lady, my mouth watering for a tall glass of the wonderful tangy drink sweetened with real sugar. We hadn't had anything but honey or sorghum molasses since war was declared, and sugar and flour were hard to come by.

I sadly thought of the lemonade Mama used to make for me. But it was more than the memory of her lemonade that made me sad. I'd hear an old song Mama used to sing or smell lilacs she loved to grow, and I'd be biting my tongue, holding back the clouds.

At least we were back in Pine Bluff after spending such a miserable time in Little Rock. Daddy had moved us away from all we knew and married a woman who couldn't get along with the angel Gabriel, himself.

I didn't miss all the feuding that went on between Daddy and his wife, Miss Rhodie Schneider, as she still called herself. But, I did miss her housekeeper, Lethie, who talked to me as if I was a person with some value. I knew she was thinking about us right now, wondering if we were eating right or minding our manners. She had a good heart, much like Mama, who was taken away from us long before her time. It was hard to understand death at seven years old, but I remembered Mama's well. I also remembered the whole family suffering after she left us.

CHAPTER 2

LOVE AND LOSS, PINE BLUFF 1912

"Stop snoring, Ella!" Nola moaned, punching me in the ribs as she sat up all huffy and mad. I squinted at my chubby little five year old sister rolling to the other side of our shared bed. Only a moment ago, my dead Mama had perched above me, disappearing in a mist.

"Be my big girl," Mama had whispered. "Daddy's going off to work for a while, but I'm satisfied you'll be just fine. Now, don't you worry, Sister."

I jumped up and looked at Daddy's wall calendar. Today said Sunday, May 9, 1912. Monday was circled, the day he was scheduled go back to his job at the Cotton Belt Railroad. A shiver of lonesomeness went through me just as Daddy knocked at the door.

"Time to rise and shine, girls," he said soft and low.

I hurried to take my long johns off and pulled a dress over my head. I glanced at Nola. She lay there sucking on her thumb like a baby, playing like Mama wasn't really gone.

I dabbed a cloth in the water on the washstand. The coldness shocked me, and that wasn't all. When I looked in the mirror, I saw Mama's face in my own. Hazel eyes, turned up nose like Mama's, thick almost black hair and what Mama called an olive skin. I promised myself to wear a bonnet outside today. Mama had told us girls to cover ourselves so we wouldn't turn too dark. Mama hadn't wanted our shameful Indian blood to show.

"Get up, Nola!" I yelled as I picked up the hairbrush, and then put it down again. No time for getting the snarls out now. Daddy was ready for me, the Rock, to make some biscuits.

He read the *Arkansas Gazette* as I walked into the kitchen. He ran a hand over my head of disheveled hair as I passed him.

"Did the rats play in your hair last night, Ella?" he asked, apparently thinking I would laugh.

"No, sir," I said soberly as I pulled my stool over to the cabinet and got the bread bowl down. Biscuit making was my job in the mornings, even though I had to stand on a stool to reach the counter. I glanced at the wood stove to see if the heat was about right.

"You're good at that, Sister. When you first started cooking, your bread was hard as rocks!" Daddy said, and the skin around his sparkling pale blue eyes crinkled as he chuckled.

"Yes, sir," I said avoiding his gaze.

"Sister, Daddy knows how hard it is for you," he said, as though he was talking about a daddy in another room.

"I'm seven years old, not a baby," I said.

"You'll always be my baby girl, Ella. That's why I want to take some of the load of caring for little Daniel off you. This morning I took him to Aunt Leah's, and she's going to keep him when I'm working."

Daniel was our two-month-old baby brother who had caused Mama to die.

"He'll be fine with us. I'm the one who knows how to give him his milk," I said as meanly as I could.

"You'll be busy taking care of yourself," Daddy said. "Besides, lots of people have offered to help us out. Grace Harlen and Mary Louise Terrill both said they'd be much obliged to watch Daniel."

"Mama wouldn't like that, Daddy," I said boldly. "Mama said Mrs. Terrill is always feigning illness, and Mrs. Harlen is a busy-body."

Daddy sucked in his breath hard so I could hear his hatred of my words. I knew he was holding his temper in, but I was so mad at him for leaving us tomorrow that I tried to rile him some more.

"And Mama said neither one of them has a chick nor a child. So, Daddy, how do they know how to take care of a baby?"

"Leave it be, Ella," he said. "Just finish your cooking."

I put the last biscuit in the pan, and Daddy walked over to the window and peered out.

"Are those boys going to finish milking or not?" he boomed, mostly for my benefit.

My two brothers could get so distracted out there in the cow lot. They squirted milk at the cat or threw cow patties at each other more than they got to the serious business of milking Pokey, our milk cow.

I just couldn't imagine how we four young slackers were going to make it without a parent around. Then I remembered my other misery and started thinking about Mama again.

I closed my eyes for a minute to see if I could still remember her in the casket. The image wouldn't come.

What did come was a vision of Daddy. When Mama died, he went out on the back porch by himself. He strummed his guitar and hummed low and sad. Then, without apology, he put his head in his hands and wept.

"Mama's gone to heaven," he said as he gathered us in his arms. He was holding on to baby Daniel, tiny and squirming.

McKinley and Dewey backed away, but Nola and I stood as close to Daddy as we could.

"Where is heaven?" Nola asked.

"It's a place where God lives, and it's a happier place than where we are right now," he said.

"But, I like it here," I said. "Why did Mama want to go to heaven?"

"This life is just a rehearsal of what real life will be like in heaven," he said, as he struggled with the baby.

"Take Daniel," he said, handing him over to me. I looked down into the tiny face, red with the wretchedness of crying.

"You're my rock, Ella," he said. "I don't know how I'd manage without you."

It was a nice thing to say, but it didn't fool me much. I knew Daddy had no other choice since I was the oldest girl and this was woman's work. I didn't care either way because I liked Daniel. No, really, I loved Daniel.

I began to snuggle him close and rock back and forth, and his eyelids fluttered and closed. Then I knew for sure that I was his and he was mine.

McKinley was the oldest kid, twelve years old, always outgrowing his shoes and heading upward to Daddy's height. He continually talked about quitting school and going to work at the diamond mine in Murfreesboro. Daddy frowned hard when McKinley talked about it. Then he would stare directly into McKinley's eyes and tell him he wasn't about to quit school and go to work anywhere.

Dewey was nine and next in age to McKinley. He couldn't sit still and was always getting into trouble with Daddy. Where McKinley was Daddy's look-alike with blue eyes and black hair, Dewey's hair was kissed by the sun, and his freckles fit perfectly on a face full of mischief. Then there was Nola, only five, and baby Daniel, just a few weeks old with no mama to feed him.

Nola and I looked a lot alike with dark hair and short sawed-off bodies. Her almost-black hair lay in lazy curls, while mine was fine and straight.

Mama's sister, Aunt Leah, lived across the road. Her daughter, Katherine, whom we called Kit, was my only cousin and closest friend. They had both come to the house every day while Mama was sick.

Then my poor mama, half-asleep and feverish, had held out her hands to little Daniel for the last time. Losing so much blood had made Mama powerless, and finally, there was no more air in the room left for her to breathe.

CHAPTER 3

SAYING GOODBYE

"Get Nola and the boys, and go to my house," Aunt Leah told me. "Warm up the soup for you children. Boil some milk, and let it cool for the baby. I'll show you how to feed it to him with a spoon."

"Yes ma'am," I said, opening the door and inhaling the smell of the night's rain. The scent of new growth on pine trees sent me into a sneezing fit as I stumbled across the porch, turning my ankle as I stepped into a hole. I was in such a stupor it didn't even hurt at the time. I wondered how I would be the Rock that day.

Little, skinny Dewey had dibs on carrying Daniel because I was crippled. I hobbled along behind him holding Nola's hand. McKinley followed with his head down, kicking dirt clods. I'll never forget the smell of that misty day and the honeysuckle and the wet dirt.

Daddy came to Aunt Leah's at twilight to walk us home. Usually, it was my favorite time of evening. But not today, because I dreaded walking into that sad house with my heavy heart and throbbing ankle.

Two whole days before the burial, Mama lay in a pine coffin in the parlor. Aunt Leah had placed the pearl-edged combs in her hair and a soft pink gown on her body. She looked like she was sleeping.

I picked up Mama's hand, but put it down fast. It was hard and cold, not soft like the hands that had brushed my hair a hundred strokes a night.

Now, I can't remember the funeral at all. I can just see Nola and me behind the wagon crying and holding on to each other.

The next few days, I warmed milk and fed it to baby Daniel with a spoon. Daddy left most of Daniel's care to the boys and me. Now, I didn't mind the responsibility; I just wanted Mama back.

One morning Daddy asked everyone to take a seat at the kitchen table with him.

"Children, the railroad needs me at work. I don't want to leave you, but I have to put food on the table. When I go back next week, Aunt Leah and her friends, Mrs. Harlen and Mrs. Terrill, will watch Daniel for us."

He stopped for a moment and looked at McKinley. "And you boys will be in charge here at the house."

"Why can't we stay with Aunt Leah?" I whined as I looked at the calendar with the days marked off for Daddy's work. Nola and I would be under the boys' rule forever and ever!

"Leah's house is not big enough for two families, Sister. But you know she's right across the road anytime you have a problem."

"We stay by ourselves?" said Nola. "What if we get scared?"

"If you're afraid, just think about your daddy firing that train engine. Every time you hear a whistle, that's me with you in spirit."

Nola looked down at her feet, and a tear dribbled down her face.

"Get the guitar for me, Nola, and come here. Let's sing; it'll make us feel better."

She took him the guitar. He took it lovingly, almost reverently. Maybe it was because it was the only possession he had salvaged from his sad childhood in Georgia.

He held it like a precious jewel and began to strum it. Nola laid her head on his knee and put her thumb in her mouth.

"There's a church in the valley by the wildwood......." he sang. Daddy's voice boomed, and for a moment, everything seemed right again. Then my heart started pounding in my ears, and I wanted Mama back.

CHAPTER 4

ON OUR OWN

The next day Daddy hitched our team of mules to the wagon and took us to Dalby Brothers Store to pick up groceries. He bought enough to last us until he got back home. Daddy didn't realize that we were serial eaters and everything in sight would be devoured long before he returned from the railroad.

Nola wept when he slung the bag over his shoulder to leave.

"When you get little and I get big, I'm gonna run off to the railroad and leave you!" she cried pitifully. Daddy stroked the top of her head and looked over at me solemnly.

"Why don't you two go over to Leah's and check on Daniel?" he said. Then we watched him as he started toward Union Station.

I grabbed Nola's hand and pulled her toward Aunt Leah's.

"Don't watch him walk down the road," I said. "Kit says it's bad luck to look at somebody leave."

"Daddy says Kit is just thuperthithous," she said - her version of 'superstitious' with a lisp. But she took heed to the silly notion and started running over to Aunt Leah's full speed ahead, not looking back at Daddy walking.

At Aunt Leah's, Daniel recognized us; we could see that. I took him to his pallet on the floor and started playing with him. Nola and I told each other how smart he was as he made gurgling noises and blew little bubbles. His eyes focused mainly on me, though.

"Danny's got little red curls," I cooed at him. "You're pretty enough to be a girl."

He smiled and tried to focus his eyes. Then, he began kicking his legs excitedly.

"What's he doing, Aunt Leah?" Nola asked.

"Daniel's just learning to exercise." She laughed.

He began rubbing his eyes and getting squirmy. Aunt Leah made a face and wrinkled her nose because he had a dirty diaper. She cleaned him up and took him out on the front porch to rock.

Nola called me over to look at a Sears & Roebuck catalog she found on the table.

"I'm gonna buy me a pretty red dress when I get big. I'm gonna ride in one of them automobiles too," she said.

"That'll be the day," I said as our cousin Kit came out of her room.

"Where's Mama?" she asked, looking around for Aunt Leah. "Let's ask if we can spend the night together."

"She's out on the porch," I told her. "Kit, stay at our house tonight. It'll help us get used to being there alone without Daddy for the first time."

The three of us walked out on the porch. Aunt Leah was rocking back and forth, and Daniel was sound asleep.

"Will you let Kit spend the night with us?" I asked. She hesitated a moment while adjusting Daniel in her lap. I hoped she would say yes, but her husband, Uncle Josh, was working day and night at the lumber mill. She liked Kit around because she was Aunt Leah's rock like I was Daddy's.

"Yes, if you children behave yourselves. Remember to include Nola in your games; she gets lonesome too. And tonight at bedtime, no telling ghost stories."

"Yes ma'am," I said and hugged her. She pulled me close and then held me in front of her, staring into my face.

"You are your mama made over," she said, and hugged me again. "Kit, go get the brush. I want to fix you girls' hair. I don't think you've brushed it in a month of Sundays."

I looked at Aunt Leah closely. Her brown hair was pulled up on her head in a bun made of braids. Her eyes were light brown and twinkly like she knew a pretty secret.

"Aunt Leah, that feels good," I said as she brushed and brushed. "You're putting me to sleep."

"I'll fix your hair anytime," Aunt Leah said kindly. "Just ask."

When she finished with me, she brushed Nola's hair until it got big on her head with curls fluffing out everywhere. I started laughing.

"Little girl with the big head!" I teased.

She spit fire from her eyes and started to slap at me, but missed.

"All right, girls, you're all fixed now," Aunt Leah said calmly. "You can run on over to your house. Don't make messes, and don't be noisy. If you need me, little Daniel and I'll be right here!"

"I'm sorry, Nola," I said, seeing she was swatting at me again. "Your hair is fine."

After we Eskimo kissed Daniel, we started across the road to our house. That's when it hit me that our house was a mess!

The porch sagged, the paint was cracking, and the door looked like it wanted to fall off. Mama would have fainted if she had seen that yard. It was the boys' job to keep it neat and clear of objects, not jumbled up with trash. Mama liked her house and yard very neat and clean.

As usual, the boys had gone to the Arkansas River to fish, so we decided to right their wrong. We gathered up tin cans and stacked them high in two rows to make the sides for a room. Then we made a ceiling out of lumber planks. We called our creation a schoolhouse, and Kit pretended to be a teacher. She was the most qualified because she was a year older than I was and usually the bossiest anyway.

Nola and I were her students. We wrote on slates with chalk, and recited pretend lessons. We worked hard for about half an hour, and then Nola got bored with being still, so we turned in our slates and chalk to our teacher. I could tell Miss Kit wasn't ready to end the school day, but when her students left the premises, she announced class was over in a loud voice.

We went inside our house. For the rest of the day, we ate walnuts Daddy had shelled and roasted for us. We also had cheese, hardtack, pickles, and candy. I didn't make a biscuit, not one, and wouldn't until we ran out of the real goodies. The dishes sat waiting for the flies to find them.

The boys came home empty-handed except for their fishing poles. I didn't want to fry fish anyway. Instead, we all ate more snacks and went to the cow lot to watch the boys milk. Kit liked to watch them in action.

McKinley warned us to look out for snakes, but I was more afraid of mice. McKinley said that our cat, Callie, would see to the mice, so not to worry.

Kit was a bigger scaredy-cat than I was. She stepped lightly. She screamed when tall grass blew in the wind or a curly tree branch got in her way.

"Dewey, you milk first," McKinley said. "Then I'll finish and let the calf have its turn on the other side of Pokey."

Pokey was our Jersey milk cow, and Daddy had gotten her because Jerseys make the richest cream. Since Pokey chewed her cud day and night and cows are supposed to have several stomachs, I could see why her milk was so creamy.

Dewey did everything fast. He grabbed the bucket, set it under Pokey, and began squeezing and pulling on her udders. Streams of fresh milk began floating in the bottom of the bucket, making foam. Callie showed up, and Dewey was happy to squirt a drink toward her mouth, but of course, it hit her in the eye.

She was not to be defeated though and instantly jumped back into the race for a second turn.

"Bud, that's enough," McKinley said and grabbed the pail. He stomped his foot for Callie to scat, and she ran lickety-split out of the cow lot. Dewey got Pokey's calf to go to her other side and start nursing. She was clearly a hungry calf; she was gulping and couldn't suckle fast enough.

"Want us to collect the eggs?" Kit asked. She was always happy to do these chores because she wasn't allowed to gather eggs at home.

"Sure, there's a basket in the corner," McKinley said. I could already see McKinley was playing up his role as the man in charge.

While Pokey chewed her cud and donated her milk, we three girls went to gather the eggs. We had one rooster and three hens, but only one hen would cooperate and lay eggs.

Kit had the basket and reached her hand into the nest. She pulled her hand back and made a disgusted noise. When she saw it was a chicken snake, she screamed bloody murder and dropped the basket. Then she grabbed McKinley, who almost spilled the bucket of milk.

Dewey started laughing and jumping around. Then he looked into the nest and saw a big snake with a lump bulging in its middle about the size of an egg. His eyes got bigger than half dollars, and he ran behind Pokey.

I grabbed the hoe. As the snake slithered down the side of the chicken coop, I smacked it as hard as I could. It kept slithering, so Dewey grabbed the hoe and smacked it again, but it got away with one of our eggs in itself.

"I'm not eating any more eggs," Nola whined.

"Silly, you don't eat the shell anyway," Dewey said.

"Snakes are poison," she said, "and I don't want to eat poison."

McKinley started a long talk about how some snakes are poison and others aren't. He allowed that chicken snakes are not. His explanations took forever, another reason I daydreamed.

Kit stood still and speechless. I thought that if she were afraid of attacking an enemy like a snake, she would never make a school-teacher.

That night the boys got out the fiddle and guitar and started making music. I asked McKinley to play "Wildwood Flower," and he started picking. Then Dewey joined in with Daddy's fiddle, which just about covered his whole body.

Kit and I began to harmonize, and Nola tried to join in:

"I'll think of him never; I'll be wildly gay
I'll charm every heart and the crowd I will sway.
I'll live yet to see him regret the dark hour,
When he won, then neglected the frail wildwood flower."

I tapped my feet and tossed my head back and forth to the rhythm. Music was in me, and singing was my first love. I guess much of it came from Mama. She used to hum and sing all day long while she sewed dresses for Nola and me. She said it seemed to make her chores easier and today when I sing with my brothers playing their instruments, I hear her sweet, perfect voice in my mind. Her songs were a mixture of lilting Scottish music combined with a tinge of bittersweet Ozark and they sounded oh so sad.

The boys were good at their music, especially McKinley. He would first say what key they were playing in and begin tapping his foot. Then Dewey would put the fiddle to his chin and aim his bow at the strings.

Daddy taught McKinley the guitar, but Dewey had to take fiddle lessons. McKinley impatiently told him to rosin the bow when his notes got squeaky.

As the evening wore on, we girls danced around to "Arkansas Traveler," and "Pretty Red Wing," and then I sang "Swing Low, Sweet Chariot," by myself while the boys played. When McKinley stopped to tune his guitar, I knew the fun was over. He spent many an hour trying to get that guitar to sound just right.

"Let's go into the kitchen and do something else," I said.

"Okay, here's a riddle," Kit said as she sat down in a dining chair and looked at Nola and me.

"Abe Lincoln asked this one time. How many legs does a mule have if you call a tail a leg?"

"Five!" Nola shouted.

"Do you agree, Ella?" Kit asked.

"Yep, five," I said.

"Wrong," Kit said. "The answer is four. Calling a tail a leg doesn't make it a leg."

"That's a stupid riddle," Nola whined.

"It's just a game, Nola," I said. "Okay, I have one. What happens when you cross a chicken and a dog?"

"Umm, I don't know. What?" Kit asked.

"You get pooched eggs," I said, and we all giggled.

"My turn," said Nola. "Why did the kid cut down the tree?"

"You tell us," said Kit.

"Because he was knotty (naughty)," Nola said, very proud of herself.

Soon we ran out of riddles, so I pulled out a piece of twine and began to make a Jacob's ladder with my fingers. Then Kit showed Nola how to make crow's feet, and Nola got all tangled up in the string. Dewey came by, took the string, and pretended to choke her. He got the response he wanted and Nola shoved him and screamed.

"Time for bed!" McKinley yelled, very perturbed.

"Tell me a story like Daddy does!" squealed Nola.

"Not tonight," McKinley said. "We need to get to sleep."

We got ready for bed, and I climbed into the middle with Nola on one side and Kit on the other. I lay stiff as a poker to make us all fit. Suddenly, something crashed outside the window. It wasn't the boys; they were tuning guitar strings. More clangs.

I clutched the arm of each girl. I held my breath so hard my cheeks puffed out. I glanced at the bright moon through the window. Then I saw the image of a face looking through our window.

CHAPTER 5
MAKING THE BEST OF THINGS

Suddenly a noise like crashing cymbals shattered the silence. I held my breath, frozen to my spot in bed. Then I saw a man staggering by the window once again. I closed my eyes tight.

Tap, tap, tap went something on the other side of our door. Nola put her head under the cover, and Kit held on to me for dear life.

When no one answered the knock, McKinley and Dewey threw open our door.

"What in the Sam Hill did you do that for?" McKinley asked meanly.

"Do what for?" I whispered, barely opening my eyes.

"Set those cans and boards up outside where someone could collide into them?"

We all jumped up and looked out the window and saw a man staggering down the street.

"Was that a robber?" asked Nola.

"Ha ha ha ha," Dewey laughed. "Scared you, didn't it?"

"No, dumbo, it wasn't a robber," said McKinley. "It was just an old man. Now, why did you do that?"

"We just made a schoolhouse," Kit said, confused, as she got back into bed. "What was wrong with that old man that he had to come into our yard?"

"Your schoolhouse just about scared that poor old thing to death, Kit. He had too much moonshine and came stumbling by and ran into those cans. He nearly jumped through his hat."

Kit began giggling; then I began giggling, and Nola started laughing too.

"That's what he gets for drinking that old nasty whiskey," said Kit.

"Amen," I said. "Let's go to sleep."

We all settled down then. The other two fell asleep fast, but I lay listening for Daddy's train. I asked God if he would forgive us for scaring that man. I closed my eyes, and a train whistled. My heart thumped in my ears, and I hoped Mama would visit me in my dreams.

But, Mama didn't come. Nor did anything change for two weeks without Daddy. Kit spent several nights with us, and we did the best we could with what we had. One night we made music till late.

When I got up the next morning, the fire was blazing in the cook-stove, and coffee was made. McKinley and Dewey stood by the table arguing. I made me a cup of coffee milk just as Dewey started to take a swing at McKinley.

"What's wrong with you two?" I asked, eyeing the checker-board and checkers scattered all over the floor.

"McKinley's a cheater!" Dewey said as McKinley got him in a head-lock.

"I'm telling," I said. "Daddy said for you not to fight."

McKinley let Dewey go and whacked him on the shoulder. Dewey started jumping around as if he was hurt. But instead of complaining, he started laughing and taunting McKinley.

"You're so ugly; you look like you've been whipped with an ugly stick."

"You're so ugly…" McKinley said.

I opened the door to go outside so I could get away from the rift. I never understood how boys could be friends one minute, hit around on each other, and say the worst insults, and then be buddies again.

I walked across the porch to the steps and sat down with my coffee milk. Dewey came out the door, slamming it as always, and bounced his way over to me.

"Want to go fishing today, Sister?" he asked.

"I thought you were in the middle of a fight," I said.

"We were just joshing each other," Dewey said. "Besides, McKinley was ready to go out and milk, and I made a deal with him to get out of it this morning."

"What kind of deal?"

"Paid him off. Gave him some change I've been saving. Now, do you want to go fishing or not?"

"Naw, I want to play with Kit," I said.

"She can go with us."

"We'll see," I said, just like my daddy said it, and looked off past the front gate. I saw the figure of a man on down past Aunt Leah's walking toward our house. I squinted to make out who it was. I hoped it was Daddy, but Daddy wouldn't be carrying a gun.

"Here comes Charlie Wright," Dewey said, kicking a can across the yard.

Charlie was somewhat older than McKinley, but he didn't act like any boy I'd ever seen. He muttered to an imaginary enemy, or he choked up with fits of laughter, with not much breathing space in between. He carried a little cloth sack full of tobacco and papers to roll cigarettes. If he wasn't smoking one, he was rolling one. When he wasn't smoking or rolling one, he was coughing.

Mama had told me not to be afraid of Charlie. He was beaten up by some drifter cotton pickers, and it damaged his brain. When he got a case of nerves, he took his twenty-two rifle outside, pointed it up to the sky, and shot two or three times.

Nola was scared of him, but I wasn't. She didn't understand his talking in Spanish sometimes. As for me, when he said "*que pasa*," I looked him straight in the eye and said "*que pasa*" right back. I knew some of the hands on Charlie's parents' place spoke Spanish, and he probably learned it from them. Sometimes Charlie used bad words when he got to thinking about those people. He shouted at them, loud and mean, as though they were in the air! It's true he often got angry at these invisible strangers, but he never got mad at us.

Mama had said Charlie was one of God's angels, and I gave him credit for that.

But today I wasn't in the mood for company. Besides, tin cans were all over the place, and I knew Charlie would have something odd to say about them.

"Whatcha doin' out so early?" Dewey asked.

"Looking for squirrels," he muttered. "They're taking over the walnut trees."

"Charlie, you can put your gun inside the door," McKinley said, walking hurriedly in from the cow lot. "Ella is just about to start breakfast."

He looked over at me with a nod.

I got up slowly, making an effort to show I was being put upon.

"All right," I sighed, acting really tired, "I'll make an extra pan of biscuits."

"That would be nice, Sister," Charlie said. I stepped into the house and sighed. Why in tarnation did he have to call me *Sister* too?

I got the bread pan down and yelled at Nola. "Get in here and fix the eggs!" The one chore she could do well was crack and scramble eggs.

Nola came in as far as the fireplace and sat down.

"I'm not touching any poison eggs," she moaned. She sucked her thumb and stared at the gun by the door.

"Then we're not having eggs," I said, miffed, just as McKinley walked in.

"Sister, just forget the eggs. Nola, you don't have to worry. Charlie just wants some company," McKinley said. "Don't hurt his feelings. He's on the porch watching for squirrels."

McKinley could sure talk a good game when he wasn't the one being put upon.

In the meantime Dewey was bouncing around like a rubber ball in the yard. He kicked a can pretending it was a ball. Charlie smoked and coughed and watched for squirrels. I could hear it all amid my own banging of pans.

Kit came into the kitchen in her gown, and I told her she better get her dress on.

"We've got company," I said pointing to the door.

"Who is it?" she said.

"Charlie Wright," I said and pointed to the gun.

Kit twirled her finger around at the side of her temple indicating that somebody was not right in the head.

"Loco coco," she said.

"No sense in us making fun of him," I said a little self-righteously. "Daddy said only by the grace of God does one thing happen to a person, and something else to another. Besides, we'll eat breakfast, and it won't take long for him to get bored with us."

"Well, aren't you a Goody-Two-shoes!" she said. "He gives me the woolies."

"Don't be afraid of Charlie. He can't help what's wrong with him," I said. But, I had to admit I was a little uneasy around Charlie at times.

Kit helped me finish making breakfast. She eyed Charlie suspiciously when he came inside.

"Umm, them biscuits shore smell good," he said and sat down in Daddy's chair.

"He sounds like he's from somewhere up in the Ozarks," Kit whispered as she picked up the bowl of gravy to take to the table. If he heard her, Charlie didn't react.

He looked a mess. He wore his shirt-tail out over his khaki pants and made a stab at combing his hair, but it didn't slick down right. His fingers were stained dirty yellow from nicotine. The lucky thing for Charlie was he didn't know he was a mess. Right that minute all he cared about was food.

Dewey served himself first and then passed the biscuits and gravy around. He wouldn't have filled his own plate first if Daddy were here.

Charlie ate like he was starved.

"Got any butter, Sister?" Charlie said, and I was again annoyed. Not only had I forgotten to let the cream rise on the milk and churn the butter, but Charlie was calling me Sister again.

"No," I told him, "but we have some pear preserves."

That suited him, and he asked Kit if she wanted some. She shook her head no, and quickly looked down at her plate.

It was obvious Kit was skeptical of Charlie. Also, she'd been frightened out of her wits by the playhouse disaster and chicken snake yesterday.

As we ate, the boys kept forking more biscuits off the plate in the center of the table. We girls ate very little, and suddenly there was only one piece of bread left on the plate.

Charlie forked it.

"Charlie Wright, don't you know it's bad luck to take the last piece of bread?" Kit said.

"Well, now," he said. "I don't expect I'll have bad luck any worse than I've already had, so I think I'll just eat it anyway."

He laughed sheepishly, and looked around the table. Kit cleared her throat and threw her napkin on her full plate of food.

"Kit, do you want to play jump rope this morning?" Nola chimed in, attempting to keep the peace, and cheer her up.

"Sure." she said. Kit got up very quickly and left her breakfast sitting there. She didn't smile and stiffly followed Nola out the door.

I gathered up the dishes and put them in the dishpan. I let them soak in water and lye soap flakes. It was hard living up to my nickname of the Rock sometimes, being put upon and all.

I walked toward the barn and saw Pokey nibbling on grass while her calf was trying to nurse. Pokey was trying to escape from her responsibility, and I knew how Pokey felt.

The odor from the cow lot would make a city girl sick, but the combination of hay and manure made me feel at home, because I had always been around it. Besides, we used the manure for fertilizer to raise vegetables in the spring. This year we hadn't planted a garden because we lost Mama.

Charlie came toward the barn to do his smoking and coughing. I found our big, thick jump rope, and Charlie offered to swing it for us. Beggars can't be choosers, so we said yes. Kit tied the rope to the side of a barn door, and Charlie began to swing it. First Kit ran into it and jumped twenty-seven times. Then Nola tried, but her short legs couldn't make it over.

I jumped thirty-two times, but it made my stomach hurt. It was all those biscuits and lumpy gravy playing ball in my stomach. I plopped down on an old milking stool and watched Kit go again.

Suddenly Charlie swung around and said, "Let me get my gun!"

Kit stopped in her tracks and said she had to go home, but I caught her arm.

"Charlie won't hurt us. He's looking for squirrels."

"I don't see any out here," Kit said looking confused.

Charlie was back in a flash. Nola was standing behind me holding on to my dress, and Kit was standing as close as she could.

Charlie shot into the air and said some ugly words I'd heard only once or twice.

"What's wrong, Charlie?" I screamed.

"They're after me," he said.

"Who's after you?" I asked.

"Them cotton pickers are flying around saying bad things to me."

"Are them cotton pickers like birds?" Nola asked.

"No, but they fly around behind the buzzards, and you know what seeing a buzzard means," said Charlie.

"I don't," said Kit, looking afraid.

Still looking into the sky with his gun pointing upward, he told us all about his theory on buzzards. Charlie was big on superstition, and Kit was bound to pick up his superstition and run with it.

"Buzzards. One's sorrow, two's joy, three's a letter, and four's a boy. Five's silver, and six is gold; seven's a secret that's never been told. Eight's a date, nine's a ring, and ten's a wedding in the spring." He started laughing in a high-pitched tone, and then he coughed until he was bent over, trying to get his breath.

"What's so funny, Charlie?" I asked.

"Oh, I hardly ever see eight or nine or ten buzzards together. Usually, it's just one or two."

"And the cotton pickers are with it?" Kit asked.

"Well, now, let's talk about something else," he said, and slowly put down the gun. I saw Kit looking at me with a deadpan face.

"He gets an 'incomplete' on his report card," stated teacher Kit.

"Hee hee hee hee hee," Charlie snickered, getting the humor.

Kit fidgeted and looked squeamish. Truly none of us could make any sense of Charlie sometimes, but I knew we would never see buzzards in the sky again without counting them.

Dewey and McKinley took their time checking on us. Finally McKinley came to ask Charlie to come to the house.

"Let's make some music, Charlie," he said.

"Ah, music," Charlie said, looking into the distance. "Ain't that the great equalizer in human relationships?"

"Ith'nt, not ain't, Charlie," Nola corrected in her lisp.

"Okay, ith'nt," he said laughing shrilly as we all walked to the house.

The next thing I knew they were playing their instruments, and Kit was hightailing it home on the double.

I told Nola to come on with me, but she said she had wet her underpants. I took her inside and gave her a good talking to just like Mama or Aunt Leah would do. I told her all she had to do was ask me, and I would take her to the outhouse. So we had to find her some dry clothes and clean her up.

The boys were still playing music on the porch, so I went out and started gathering up the tin cans.

"Be sure and put those cans over there," McKinley said, pointing to the trash barrel. I turned and gave him my meanest look.

"I'll help you, Sister," Charlie said, and put down Daddy's banjo he'd been playing. Then he burped about the loudest burp I'd ever heard.

"Charles Wright, what in the world did you do that for?" I asked him. "No wonder people think you're—."

Charlie cut in. "Sister, how would you feel if everybody thought you were crazy?" he asked.

He put down his instrument, picked up his gun, and stomped off. He threw open the gate and walked out, leaving it wide open.

Nola ran to shut it. Daddy was a stickler for having the gates and doors closed.

"Why'd he leave this open?" she said, real grown uppity.

"Well, he's just Charlie." I said. Then everyone laughed because we all understood him and knew he had his very own agenda. But I felt heartbreak inside me for Charlie and his pitiful life.

As the sun went down that evening, I saw a figure walking toward our house. I hoped it was Daddy coming home and not poor Charlie coming back.

CHAPTER 6
HOME WITH DADDY

Saturday morning I opened my eyes to bright daylight. Daddy had come home the night before with good things to eat. He and the boys had made music until almost ten o'clock.

"Ella!" Daddy called from the kitchen. I rushed to pull my dress over my head and padded in to see what he wanted.

"I'll make pancakes this morning, if you churn some butter."

"Yes sir," I said and pulled out my churning jar. I looked in the crock jar where the milk rested to see if the cream had risen to the top. There it was! I dipped the cream out and into the jar. Then Daddy squeezed the lid tight, and I began churning the butter, swaying the jar back and forth, back and forth until particles of butter began to appear.

The big wood stove sang in the kitchen as Daddy sliced up salt pork for breakfast. It felt good having him back where he belonged.

"Sister, look outside. For Arkansas, this is a Georgia morning if ever I've seen one."

I looked out the window and saw the peach tree blooming. Birds fluttered around Mama's flowers, which had come back after the long winter.

"Daddy, tell me about growing up in Georgia," I said. I liked to hear about Daddy's adventures when he was a boy.

"Sister, it'll have to be a repeat, because I've told you every one of them. But I'll start off at the beginning."

"My parents and I were living in Dallas, Georgia. One day the world turned black, and the wind started raging. Ma and Pa were standing on the porch deciding whether we should go to the cellar, and a big bolt of lightning struck both of them. They didn't live to tell about it, and all that was left of us was me and Pa's guitar that I still play."

"My grandparents took me home with them to their plantation. A plantation is a farm, Sister. Anyway, my grandma and grandpa still had about a dozen sons at home. Those boys were so lazy they made me their slave. In other words, they bossed me around and gave me the work they didn't want to do."

"Like what?" I asked.

"Like going to the gristmill on Saturdays, or cleaning out the pigpen, or scooping up manure for the garden. By the time I was thirteen, I started thinking about how I was going to run away."

"Were you afraid?" I asked, still churning my butter.

"Sister, I was afraid to go but more afraid to stay. I was an old thirteen because I'd been through a lot of hard times. Anyway, one day I took the corn down to the gristmill to be ground. With it I took my fishing pole, my guitar, and a plan."

He turned and began pouring the pancake batter into the iron skillet. It sizzled and smelled good.

"What was your plan?" I asked.

"I aimed to run off where nobody could ever find me. So, I went to the river and threw in my fishing pole. Then I tossed my hat on top of it, slung my guitar over my shoulder, and started walking. I kept on walking through the brush and swamp till I ended up on a Mississippi riverboat as a cabin boy."

"Those were the days," he said softly. "Everybody petted me because as far as they knew I had no family. I stayed on that boat so long that I worked my way up to being the cook."

"Didn't your grandparents look for you?" I asked.

"I'm sure they thought I'd drowned. At least they never found me," he said.

"I'm glad they didn't find you, Daddy." I said. "Or you would still be working on that plantation, and you wouldn't have us!"

He smiled and watched me finish churning.

"It's about ready, Daddy," I said and put the butter into a mold. I saved the buttermilk for Daddy and the boys. When they drank it, Nola and I both held our noses and said pew-ee!

By then the room was filled with smells of pork and pancakes and coffee boiling on the stove. McKinley and Dewey followed their noses to the kitchen.

"Tell me about when you and Mama met," I said, ignoring the boys.

"I met your mama right here in Pine Bluff after I started working for the railroad. When I met her, I thought I'd never seen a prettier woman in my life. She had a beautiful heart too."

"Her mother was Cherokee and came to Arkansas when the Indians' land was taken from them about 1840. Her papa was a redheaded Scottish-Irish fellow who came from the old country and ended up here. They met in Greenbriar, about forty miles from here, and later moved to Pine Bluff. They just had two children: your mother, Rebeccah, and your Aunt Leah."

"Why did the Cherokees let those people take their land?" I asked.

"The Cherokees were duped, in my opinion," he continued on. "Gold deposits were found on their land, and not long after that, those federal troops rounded them up and herded them at gunpoint to Oklahoma. Your mama said her mother often remembered the path they traveled, calling it *Nuna-da-ul-tsun-yi.*"

"What does that mean?" I asked.

"The place where they cried," Daddy said. He stopped and turned to me.

"Your mother was a fine woman," he said and turned back to flip a pancake. "As much as I wanted it to be different, this hard life finally got the best of your mama."

I walked over and squeezed Daddy's hand and then sat down with the boys.

"Who wants pancakes?" Daddy asked. "Call Nola in; we have a big day ahead of us. We have to do the washing and get acquainted with each other again!"

CHAPTER 7

SECOND HAND ITEMS

In the afternoon Mrs. Harlen and Mrs. Terrill rode up in a buggy. Daddy walked out the door eagerly hoping to see Daniel with them. They both came in the house talking at top speed with Daddy behind them.

Mrs. Harlen was a wide lady who wore the pants in her family. Every time her husband tried to tell a story about anything, she would correct his facts. She acted uppity, but Kit's daddy, Uncle Josh, told Aunt Leah one day she didn't have a pot to tinkle in or a window to pitch it out of.

When I told Daddy Mrs. Harlen didn't have a pot to tinkle in, he looked at me real mean.

"Sister," he sighed, "where do you come up with that strong language?"

"It's just what Uncle Josh said," I whined.

"All he meant to say was Mrs. Harlen isn't a woman of means," Daddy said.

I didn't know what "means," meant either, but I didn't dare ask.

Because Mrs. Terrill was with Mrs. Harlen, I imagined she wasn't a woman of means either. All I knew was she was a small woman who always complained of ailing. She had aches and pains and didn't mind sharing her worries with others.

I eyed the bag they brought into the house. Mama had said not to tell family business to these two ladies, because they were gossip spreaders.

"Ella, do you remember Mrs. Terrill?" Mrs. Harlen said.

"Hello, Mrs. Terrill," I said and looked down at my feet. As I looked back up at Daddy, he stared at me. He had "the look" on his face, which spoke three words: watch your manners.

"Where's our boy?" Daddy asked.

"He's over at Leah's," said Mrs. Harlen. "I'm going to pick him up on the way home and take him to my place. Jim, he's the loudest baby I've ever seen but so gloriously happy!"

I remembered again that Mama said the two ladies didn't have a chick or a child. But, they had strong convictions as to how to raise other people's children. Mama's proclamation had come right after one of their visits when Dewey was at his busiest—jumping off chairs, shouting, and constantly stirring up the grown-ups.

Mrs. Terrill came forward with an old potato sack.

"We have some clothes that our congregation collected for the children," she said, holding up a dress. "Let's see if this will be about right for you, Ella."

I felt the blood rush up my face until it tingled in my head. I didn't want her pity, and this deed made me feel poor.

"Thank you, ma'am," I said, trying to mask my feelings.

Mrs. Terrill began chattering to Daddy. "Now this isn't charity, Jim. But with losing your sweet Rebeccah, we just thought you could use the help."

"That's mighty nice of you," Daddy said. "Actually, the children and I are getting along fine, Mrs. Terrill, but we'll make good use of your kindness."

Both ladies had pleased looks on their faces, like they had done something grand.

"Would you like some coffee?" I asked, hoping they would say, "No."

"Oh no, we haven't the time," said Mrs. Harlen. "We've more deliveries to make this morning."

With that, they marched out the door, looking proud as two duchesses.

"I guess we're not the only poor people in Pine Bluff," I said to Daddy.

"Don't be mean, Sister. They're just trying to help," Daddy said.

"It's shameful to be poor," I said.

"Young lady, being poor is not a crime. Being lazy is. Now, if you keep talking like you're ashamed of your raising, I'm going to wash your mouth out with soap."

"Yes sir," I said. "But anyway, those clothes smell like mothballs."

Daddy's mouth clamped up tight like he was trying to hold words from coming out.

"We can wash out the smell. That's better than clothes being dirty, Sister. Now, call the boys in here."

"Dew!" I yelled. "Daddy needs you and McKinley!"

Daddy frowned and put his hands over his ears.

"Ella, you're getting as loud as the boys! I want you to quit being sassy. It's just not proper for a little girl to act that way."

"Yes sir," I said and went into the kitchen with my fingers crossed. No matter how charitable those ladies had been, I would never put on any of those dresses. I should have known that they would be back later with more clothes.

CHAPTER 8
AN ARKANSAS SUMMER

Months flew by and before we knew it a year had passed and another spring turned into summer. We had a routine, mainly, being lazy when Daddy was away. If we knew he was coming home, the boys started feverishly cleaning the yard and hiding plunder. Then they'd go to Aunt Leah's well and haul water over so I could wash the dishes and clean up the kitchen.

When we got bored, we roamed the streets of Pine Bluff, watching people get on and off the streetcars or wandering by the train station. In the evenings we sat with the boys, singing while they played their instruments. Nola and I both missed Mama, but when we mentioned it to the boys, they ignored us. They acted like they didn't think about her, but I didn't fall off a turnip truck. I heard Dewey sniffling sometimes after we went to bed, with McKinley telling him quietly that he felt bad too.

Most of the time the boys were on the move, though. They could only sit still when they made music. Dewey was a practical joker, and it drove McKinley to distraction. If McKinley couldn't find his hat or his ball and bat, he knew Dewey had hidden it.

"Just draw a line in the sand," he'd tell Dewey. "You cross it, and it's all over for you!"

After they wrestled around a while, they were friends again. Nola and I couldn't fight that way, as one of us ended up crying with hurt feelings.

Sometimes I walked through the house and glanced at the dirty dishes. They were stacked everywhere until someone boiled enough water to soak them. Since I was the Rock and sole washer, they only got cleansed in a crisis. Freedom was ours until we found out suddenly Daddy was on his way home or Aunt Leah was coming over.

The days were hot and humid. The Arkansas River provided us a place to do something together without disagreeing.

We each had a fishing pole. The boys made a worm bed in our back garden for bait. I would put the long stringy worms on Nola's and my hooks while she said pew-ee! She was proud to tell anyone that she'd never touched a worm.

Daddy said I was blessed with patience and had an instinct about where to fish. I could sit for long hours in the sun, wearing my bonnet, of course, and daydream my way to heaven.

We competed for catching the most fish, which I generally did. Dewey said it didn't count because most of mine were too little to eat. These perch made our stomachs much fuller that summer when the groceries ran out. Daddy made sure there was always enough meal and flour to roll them in, and we always had lard. After burning my arm, I learned to get the grease real hot and very slowly put each fish filet in the skillet. Then, I would move the iron skillet to a cooler spot to brown each piece nicely.

When Daniel was only an infant Nola and I spent long hot afternoons at Aunt Leah's. When he got to be a little older Aunt Leah had to keep him strapped in a high chair with a belt. As Mrs. Harlen said, he was a painfully loud but gloriously happy baby.

He talked baby gibber when Nola and I came into the house, holding his arms out to be held. We soon learned it was just his way of tricking us. Once he was out of the chair-jail, he got on all fours and crawled fast. He climbed and pulled buttons out of the sewing-machine drawers and ate little pieces of dirt off the floor. He tried to get up on his fat little legs, all wobbly, but would then tump over and scream to high heaven. Aunt Leah looked tired, and it was no wonder. Even we young whippersnappers couldn't keep up with his fanatic curiosity.

One visit when Daniel settled down for a nap, Kit opened her mother's trunk.

"You've got to see these pictures. I found them the other day. They're of your mother and daddy."

There was one lone picture of Mama and Daddy before they had us and newspaper articles folded and yellowed. Kit read one to us. It was written at a time Daddy had told me about called the Trail of Tears. It spoke of the Cherokee Indians and their treatment. They'd had to live and act a certain way. I couldn't imagine my mother's parents being told where they had to live and how to act.

"Then it's true what Daddy said about the Cherokees!" I said excitedly. "What else does it say, Kit?"

As she read more of the article, one silly thing the newspaper said was the Cherokees were not allowed to do the ghost dance. I didn't know what the ghost dance was; we only waltzed or square danced at our house.

According to Aunt Leah, most of Mama's aunts, uncles, and cousins went on to Indian Territory in Oklahoma. But Mama's parents stayed in Arkansas.

In their picture, Mama was short with hair down to her waist like Daddy said. Her eyes smiled, and she looked shy. Daddy was at least a head taller, and his photograph made him seem very serious. They were all dressed up in their Sunday go-to-meeting clothes.

"I'll bet they're on their way to a dance," I said.

"But not a ghost dance!" Kit said, and we all laughed, even Aunt Leah.

CHAPTER 9

ONE ROOM SCHOOLHOUSE

Remembering back to when school started that first September after Mama passed, Dewey, Mack and I started off with Nola crying because we were leaving her behind. I took her inside Aunt Leah's house and stroked her hair. I sang softly to her and promised we would be home soon. Aunt Leah told us to run on, that we would be late, and Nola would be fine.

We lived on the outskirts of town north of the city, and every child in that area attended the same school. All grades were together in one room. Again our teacher was Miss Alli Bonner, who'd moved to Pine Bluff and took room and board at Mrs. Terrill's house. Miss Bonner called her Missus Terrill, real proper-like.

Daddy said Miss Bonner was a top-notch teacher, and he was right. She taught all of us from day one.

I remember back to when I first started school and Dewey passed down his first reader to me. Now, Miss Bonner liked me because I wasn't an interrupter, so I'd taken full advantage to impress her even more. She'd told us to look at a certain page, and then she'd printed the story on the blackboard. I decided Miss Bonner would really think I was something special if I memorized the words rather than read them. When it was my turn, I stood up and looked directly into the teacher's eyes and said my memorized lines. To my surprise, she was not happy, and her blue green eyes opened wide.

I could hardly believe Miss Allibeth Bonner could scold in such a voice as she did. She also asked me to take a seat and said what I did wasn't reading. I looked across the room at Dewey to see if he was taking mental notes so he could tattle to Daddy. Not to worry; he was talking to the boy beside him as usual. I vowed then that I would always do my lessons the straight-up way.

That year one prissy girl named Molly Kay in my class began calling me names. Since the chairs were all the same size, students fit differently in them. For instance, McKinley couldn't fit under his desk very well because his legs were too long. Mine were so short that my feet just dangled in the air.

That's when Molly Kay started calling me Squatty Body and Smart Aleck.

I held my temper inside because I was an easy crier. Molly Kay wasn't going to see my tears, no siree! Miss Bonner noticed the abuse and that Molly Kay was getting other girls to not like me either. She would tell the girls to act like young ladies, please. Then she would pat me. When she wasn't nearby, they would call me Teacher's Pet.

One day I walked out of school to go home, and here Molly Kay came.

"Smart aleck!" she taunted.

"Smart aleck, yourself!" I yelled. "You're nothing but a porky pig!"

Then I grabbed her big fat arm and squeezed it hard. When she got loose, she ran off crying.

The next day she walked up to me and showed me a big bruise on her arm.

"Did I do that to your arm?" I asked.

"Yeah," Molly Kay said.

"Well, I'm glad," I said.

"That's not being very nice. My mama told me to say I'm sorry. So, there it is: I'm sorry," she said, back to her old prissy self.

"Just don't call me names anymore," I said.

"My old brother tattled on me for calling you names, and Mama said I was in the wrong."

"Did I hear you say you're sorry?" I grilled and punished her some more.

"Yes," she said. "Would you like to come spend the night with me sometime?"

I thought she was faking her sincerity, but someone must have changed her heart. She became sort of a friend, but I was secretly glad I had called her a porky because she had been so mean. She wasn't exactly wrong about me being squatty either; I was low to the ground, and I couldn't change that.

That first year back in school after Mama left was a real challenge. I had learned to be free and on my own in the summer. Now, each morning it took a half hour for the boys, Kit, and me to walk to the schoolhouse.

We got up early so the boys could milk and I could make breakfast. The boys never sloughed off on their milking chores because they were major milk drinkers.

We had to be at school by eight o'clock or Miss Bonner would lock us out. We would then have to knock on the door and be counted tardy. This only happened two times, and we promised each other we wouldn't ever get locked out again. But we were in a rush to get ready and in a slow run to get to school almost every day.

Miss Bonner brought an abacus to school for the younger children to learn to count. It was a frame with rows of beads on metal wires. We counted the beads as Miss Bonner moved them from one end to the other. As we got better at this, she would move two at once or three at once real fast, and we would have to count.

I remember when she taught us hand writing skills. She said she wanted us to concentrate on writing beautifully more than spelling right. I did as she asked, making pages full of slanted lines and swinging circles. When I learned to make letters, I thought I measured up to Dewey, but I never did match up to McKinley in handwriting. Anyway, I kept trying because I was fascinated with words.

Winter was coming and we would have plenty of time inside the house to practice our writing and arithmetic skills. It wouldn't be all that pleasant.

CHAPTER 10

COLD SPELL

E ach year turned into another like clockwork as time sped by. One winter when Daddy had been gone about two weeks we had our first cold spell. Being the kind of eaters we were, we had already run out of everything but flour, cornmeal, and potatoes. We hid our eating habits from Aunt Leah so she wouldn't report us to Daddy.

That's when I learned to make cornmeal mush. We could make a big bowl of it, put some fresh milk in it, and survive. Every breakfast, lunch and supper was cornmeal mush for a while.

One morning I got up hoping McKinley had beaten me up to make a fire. But not only was there no one up and no fire going, but there was no wood to burn. I shivered as the bitter wind showed itself through cracks in our walls. Since I only suffered through the pain of wearing my outgrown shoes at school, I tore apart an old flannel gown and wrapped a piece of it around each foot. On the way out the kitchen door, I put on a coat given to me by Mrs. Terrill.

The wind whipped me back and forth, but I finally managed to find a tree with branches to break off. My hands were raw with cold, and my nose was frozen. Even so, I managed to take a few twigs from the tree back into the house. McKinley met me at the door.

"We can't use that wood, Ella. It's wet," he said.

"It's a fine time to tell me now, McKinley. You're supposed to get up and start the fire!" I said and threw my bundle down angrily beside the fireplace.

There were neither biscuits nor cornmeal mush that day. Kit slipped over to our house with some cheese and hardtack, and Dewey milked Pokey. So, we lived through that day by staying in bed with all the covers in the house on top of us. We swore Kit to secrecy so Aunt Leah wouldn't know we'd eaten all our food.

As Mama used to say, pride goeth before the fall. When I asked McKinley what exactly that saying meant, he said our eating habits fell into that category.

"There are two kinds of the bad kind of pride," he said. "One is the kind where you start thinking you're too special. That's the kind that'll land you on your face. The second kind is like our eating habits," McKinley went on. "We have too much pride to admit to Daddy or Aunt Leah we've been eating like gluttons. Then we fall on our faces when we go hungry."

I wondered if Mama saw us right now and was saying, "Pride goeth before the fall." My stomach rumbled with emptiness. I couldn't abide cornmeal mush again, and our only hope was a miracle. I went to sleep imagining fried chicken and mashed potatoes and fresh green beans. I dreamed Mama patted me on the back. Maybe that was a sign a miracle would happen and we wouldn't be hungry tomorrow.

McKinley and Dewey got up Friday morning and milked Pokey. I was too sleepy to get out of the mound of quilts. McKinley came in and shook me.

"Get up, Sister," he said. "Daddy came home in the night. He wants you to go over to Aunt Leah's and borrow some flour."

It was a miracle! Daddy was sitting in the next room, a total surprise.

I put my feet on the cold boards beneath me. I could hear the fire crackling in the fireplace. I literally ran into the parlor and gave Daddy a quick hug as I passed by his rocker. Then I warmed my hands and turned around slowly until my long johns felt toasty. The wind had stopped howling, but ice formed inside the windows; it would be another day cooped up in the house. But, Daddy would be cooped up with us!

I went in to wake Nola, and we pulled on our dresses over our long johns. My feet were freezing, and we were both shivering. When we went back to the fireplace, Daddy had a stack of boxes in front of him.

"Here's a little something for you," he said and handed me a box. Daddy was on the sunny side of himself today, and it felt good.

"Do you have a little something for me too?" asked Nola. She was about as sweet pie, especially if there was something in it for her.

Daddy handed a box to her.

"Shoes!" we both screamed at once. Not one, but two pairs: a pair of patent leather Mary Janes for Sunday go-to-meeting days and one pair of button ups for every day.

"All luck isn't bad," I said to Nola as we went to our room to put on our stockings.

"Come on in here and model those new dancing shoes," Daddy said. I felt shy, and so did Nola somehow. When we came in, Daddy looked at us real pleased.

"Girls, I think it's time to get ready for a little party. Tell the boys to get busy telling the neighbors. We'll have a little dance here tonight. Let's get this place cleaned up."

I burst into tears. "It's too cold for a party!"

"Oh, it's supposed to warm up today, and by late evening it'll be perfect. As soon as the boys come in, we'll get our instruments tuned and make some music. That'll warm everybody up."

After I walked over to Aunt Leah's to model my new shoes for Kit and borrow flour, Daddy cooked breakfast. As we ate, I thought that heaven had come into our kitchen. I didn't forget that meal of bacon and scrambled eggs for a long time. I didn't even have to cook it either.

"Time to clean up, girls!" Daddy said.

"What about McKinley and Dewey?" Nola asked. "They ought to have to clean up too."

"That's women's work," Dewey said and tickled her ribs.

"No, now, boys, you've got your own work to do. Go get busy," Daddy said.

The boys took the wagon out and invited their friends to our dance party. It was not a problem to round up people for entertainment. Most of the natives amused themselves with music, and dancing was part of the fun. Daddy had taught Nola and me to dance while we were still young enough to place our feet on top of his shoes.

Sometimes at these parties, girls would have to dance with girls. Boys seemed to be such rascals. They would huddle over in the corner with other boys talking about ball playing or war games. My brothers were usually the instigators.

I worked all day shining up that modest little house. I barely had time to get myself spruced up before the party started. Girls swirled into the house with their desserts. They looked so beautiful to me with their hair all curled and their cheeks rosy red from the cold. The boys brought their musical instruments and came through the door teasing the girls. Kit walked over with a butter cake Aunt Leah had made, and Daddy brought out cups of hot apple cider.

Our house didn't fit the image for grand parties, but Daddy liked to have them anyway. He said it made him feel good to have young people in the house.

The fire crackled briskly. Daddy poured some vanilla extract in a pan of boiling water. The fragrance drifted through the house, making it smell as though cookies had just come out of the oven.

Nola and I were so proud of our shoes. I hoped the older girls coming in would notice our pretty feet. But they were too busy giggling with each other and looking sideways at the boys congregating in their own corner.

Dew brought out the fiddle and McKinley picked up his guitar. They started a hoedown and I grabbed Daddy before he could pick up his guitar. I liked to dance so much with Daddy that McKinley told me all my brains were in my feet. When that made me mad, Daddy said McKinley meant that I just had rhythm.

Daddy danced with me and then with Nola. Then he went over to the boys and told them to quit standing off by themselves. They needed to ask the ladies for a dance.

The night passed in a flurry of petticoats and legs tramping in the parlor of the small house. Nobody seemed to notice the imperfect walls or the cold air passing through the cracks in the floor. All the boys had traded their instruments around and all the girls had passed around their desserts. Daddy had been right; the dance warmed up the night for us.

When a train whistled low and loud, Daddy picked up Nola as if she was a baby and pulled me close to him with the other arm.

"My two little dancing girls," he said playfully. "It is real lonesome on that old train when I'm away from you."

I'd never thought about him being lonely when he was away. I'd thought it was just us.

CHAPTER 11

OPEN ARMS OF LOVE 1912

By Christmastime 1912 Nola had grown up tall for her five years and had lost a tooth. Miss Bonner promised she could start going to school in January. That was good because Aunt Leah hadn't been feeling well, and taking care of Nola didn't help

"Mama can't take care of Daniel anymore," Kit told us soberly one Sunday afternoon.

"Why?" I asked. "He loves Aunt Leah more than anyone."

"Mama's going to have a baby," Kit said.

"A real baby?" I screeched. "How do you know?"

"Look at those big blouses she's wearing the next time you see her. The baby's in her stomach," she whispered in my ear.

"Does your daddy know?" I asked.

"Well, I think so," Kit said, "because I heard him tell your daddy he's going to have to work twice as hard at the lumber mill. He said our family is getting bigger."

"Oooo, that'll be fun to have a little baby," I said. "Want to go over to Mrs. Terrill's and see Daniel?"

"Sure," she said, "but don't either one of y'all say anything about Mama's new baby."

"We won't," I said emphatically. "Aunt Leah has a right to being private."

"And that Mrs. Terrill will just want to take your baby just like she's trying to get Daniel from us," I said.

"No, Mama wouldn't allow that," Kit told us.

"I wonder why my daddy allows it," I said.

"Mama told me why," Kit said. "Your daddy couldn't take care of a little baby, being gone on the rail so much."

I kept quiet because I overheard talking between the adults sometimes. Mrs. Terrill couldn't have children, and she'd told Daddy that she and her mister wanted to raise Daniel as their own.

We stopped by Aunt Leah's to get Nola, and I glanced out of the corner of my eye at Aunt Leah's fat blouse. Kit was right. Aunt Leah was plumper.

We met McKinley coming from town in the wagon. He asked where we were going, and we told him to see Daniel, so he said to hop in; he would take us.

I think McKinley picked us up in that wagon to scare us girls to death. He drove those poor mules hard and acted like we were about to turn over. Kit and Nola started screaming. But not me; we'd played this game before, and it had mainly scared the mules.

When we got to Mrs. Terrill's house, our teacher, Miss Bonner, was on the front porch holding Daniel.

"How's my baby?" I cooed at him.

He began to jump up and down and clap his hands and say words only he could understand. I took him then, and he struggled out of my arms and showed me how he could stand alone.

"You too smart!" I said in baby talk.

"Yeth, you are!" Nola laughed and rubbed noses with him in an Eskimo kiss.

He reached over and grabbed a fistful of my hair and began to take it with him to eternity. I wrestled as hard as I could, and finally I had to pry Danny's fingers from my hair.

"No, no, Daniel," I said. "Ella needs her hair."

Daniel smiled big, showing off his two new bottom teeth. It was funny that he was just growing his in and Nola was getting hers out.

"Kit, you better get used to this," I said. "You're going to get yours pretty soon."

"Mine's going to be a little sister," she said assuredly.

"That'll be good," I said, thinking that Kit might have better luck with a baby sister.

"The Lord will give your mama and daddy the right one, no matter if it's a boy or girl," Miss Bonner said sweetly.

I smiled at her. She always knew the right thing to say, but I did wonder how she knew Aunt Leah's secret.

She touched me on the shoulder.

"Ella, women confide in each other. That's how I knew about the new baby coming," she said.

Mrs. Terrill walked out the door. "Will you come to church on Sunday, children?" she said. "There'll be dinner on the ground."

Mrs. Terrill went into great detail about the time the congregation moved out of the schoolhouse and into their first building. Of course we knew all of this because it was our church too. She went through the history of all the preachers the church had had. Then, she told us her head was splitting and told us she hoped we never hurt like this.

"What was the question you asked?" I asked, hoping Mrs. Terrill would forget she had a headache.

"Oh, I was inviting you to church on Sunday," she said, as she frowned and rubbed her temples.

"We'll try our best," I said. "Daddy's coming home tomorrow, and we'll ask him."

Mrs. Terrill turned to Miss Bonner with an eyebrow raised.

"Alli, you need to meet Jim Smith. He's their daddy and a *very* nice man."

"I met Mr. Smith when school started," Miss Bonner said coolly. "Yes, he's a nice gentleman."

"Let's all just plan to see one another on Sunday at church, then. All right, children?"

"Yes ma'am," McKinley said, and then we climbed back into the wagon. The girls waved at Daniel, who was squealing and doing a rubber-kneed little dance. Mrs. Terrill picked him up and held his hand and made it wave bye-bye.

As we drove away, McKinley said in a very low tone, "Oh me, that woman makes me tired."

"Miss Bonner?" I asked.

"No, I mean Mrs. Terrill," he said.

"Me too," I said, because Mrs. Terrill was such a complainer.

"That's okay, though," McKinley said, looking over at me. "Her heart's in the right place."

"Except she doesn't want to give us Daniel back," I said.

"Mama wouldn't like that one bit," Nola said with her frowny face on. She put her thumb in her mouth and stroked a strand of her hair.

"Don't worry about things that can't be fixed," McKinley said. "Mama's watching out for all of us."

"I want Daddy," Nola whined.

"Daddy might just be coming home with a big surprise tomorrow," McKinley said mysteriously. "I just happened to pick up a letter from Daddy at the post office."

"Tell us, tell us!" Nola and I pled.

"You'll just have to wait till school's out tomorrow," he said. "Daddy says it's a surprise we won't be able to believe!"

I thought we would die of sheer pleasure, imagining what tomorrow held for us. So, when Nola and I got ready for bed I sang one of her favorite songs to go to sleep by. She sucked her thumb as I sang, "Sleep Baby Sleep."

CHAPTER 12

DADDY'S SURPRISE

It was hard to stay focused at school the next day, thinking about Daddy's surprise. When we got home in the afternoon, we didn't see a sign of Daddy or a surprise anywhere. Nola walked over from Aunt Leah's when she saw us coming. I felt let down and threw my books on the big desk in the parlor.

"I smell his pipe!" Nola said.

"You do no such thing," I said.

"I smell somebody's pipe then," she said.

Suddenly, someone rapped on the door sharply.

"Who's that knocking at the door?" Dewey said. "Sounds like they're trying to beat it down!"

McKinley and Dewey tiptoed to the door and cracked it.

"Daddy!" Dewey said. "What are you doing out there?"

Daddy started laughing. "Come on out children; I've got a surprise for all of us. But first, give me a hug."

Nola was standing in the corner, eyes as big as saucers. "What are you so quiet about?" he asked her.

"You didn't have to shock us!" Nola said.

"Young lady, you just come out back with me, and you'll see what a shock looks like!" he said. He had a million-dollar smile on.

"Everyone close your eyes," he said.

We put our hands over our faces and squeezed our eyes shut.

"Now open them!"

There sat a brand-new shiny black Model T automobile.

"Well, what do you think?" he asked.

For once, McKinley couldn't speak. Dewey started jumping around asking whose it was, and I just stood there, tongue-tied. Not many people owned one out our way.

"Oh, Daddy, take us for a ride. Please? Pretty please with sugar on it?" Nola said.

"Let me crank it, Daddy!" Dewey yelled, jumping around.

"Dew, let me do it this time. These flivvers are tricky. People get their arms broken cranking them sometimes."

So Daddy had everyone get out of the way and climbed in through the right-hand door because there wasn't a door on the driver's side. He reached over to the wheel, set the spark and throttle levers in position, and got out to crank it. He pulled the choke and revolved the crank, and the engine roared.

We were all yelling and clapping as Daddy leapt onto the running board, moved the throttle to its proper position, and sat down at the wheel. Then we got in and went down the dirt road to town, crammed in like a bunch of sardines in a can. The cold air didn't bother me nor did Dewey's yelping as Daddy swerved to miss rocks in the road.

As we drove through town, I hoped to see Mrs. Terrill or Mrs. Harlen, who thought we were poor. I knew that was an ugly thought, but I felt it deliciously.

We almost got stuck in a rut but finally made it back to the house. The car jerked and sputtered to a stop. The smell of Daddy's pipe smoke and the gasoline sent me into a sneezing fit.

"Daddy, how did you get it home? Did you bring it to the depot on the train?" Nola asked.

"No, sweetheart, I got it at Mr. Smart's Ford dealership right here in Pine Bluff," he said looking quite proud of himself. "A pretty spiffy horseless carriage, huh, kids?"

"Or for us, a mule-less carriage," I said happily. "Will you take us to Little Rock some time?" We hadn't been very many places, and Little Rock was famous because it was the capitol of Arkansas.

"Sister, I'll be taking you many places. Right now, though, let's get the cow milked and the biscuits made for supper. We'll talk more after we eat."

Dewey and McKinley had all kinds of questions on the way home.

"How fast will it go?" McKinley asked.

"At least forty miles per hour," Daddy said.

"Wow!" said Dewey. "What are those pedals all about?"

"This one on the left is first gear, the middle one is reverse, and this one on the right is the brake," Daddy said. "You get into second gear by releasing the handbrake lever and pressing down on the left pedal."

"Daddy, when can I learn how to drive?" McKinley asked.

"While I'm home this time," Daddy said. "Right now we need to get to the house and get some supper started."

But that wouldn't happen right away. McKinley and Dewey had to look under the hood of the car to see how it worked. Dewey had to punch all the buttons and push on the pedals. Nola and I just opened and closed the doors and slid our hands over its shiny surface.

"Who ever thought a thing like this up?" Nola asked.

"Mr. Henry Ford in Detroit, Michigan," Daddy said. He's been working up there a long time, and his friend Thomas Edison invents things up there too."

"Mr. Henry Ford must be a smart man," I said.

"Yeah, and real strong too," said Nola. "If he built an automobile, he must have big muscles!"

McKinley looked at Nola with exasperation. "Nola, he has a lot of men working for him in a factory. They all put their work into it."

"Oh," Nola said, losing interest fast. "Ella, let's tell Daddy about our invitation to go to church on Sunday."

"Oh, can we, Daddy?" I said. "Miss Bonner and Mrs. Terrill said for us to be sure and come to church and have dinner on the grounds. They'll be bringing little Daniel with them."

"Okay, then, we better start baths early tomorrow," said Daddy, as we entered the house. He glanced around the back door to locate the tub we used for bathing.

The number-three washtub had fallen off its hook by the back door and rolled over against a stump. Daddy looked unhappy when he saw it coated with dirt and leaves. The boys hadn't brought water from Aunt Leah's well either. I was afraid Daddy would get onto us, so I began jabbering and making excuses.

"First, we had to get our schoolwork, then we had to see Daniel at the Terrills' house, then we had to find out about Aunt Leah's new baby that's coming, and then—"

"Just stop right there, Ella," Daddy said and didn't give me his disappointed look at all. "You all are doing the best you can without me around. Tonight let's just celebrate what we've got to be thankful about."

I was so relieved. Automobiles must make people real happy, I thought as I walked in to get the bread pan down. I noticed the boys were doing their chores quickly tonight. We ate our supper, and then Daddy put a pot of pinto beans in water to soak for cooking Saturday.

The next afternoon the boys brought buckets of water from Aunt Leah's well, and Daddy boiled it for our baths. Nola and I bathed in one tub of water, and the boys in the next one. Then Daddy made a tub for just himself.

Daddy didn't get out the guitar that night. He said he was saving his music appreciation for Sunday.

This would be one Sunday we wouldn't be walking to church. We'd be riding in a fine new automobile. So there, Mrs. Terrill!

Sunday morning we were all excited getting ready for church. Dewey was the first one dressed, and he asked me to slick down his hair. As bouncy as Dewey was, he liked to spruce up. McKinley got dressed and sat tuning his guitar and singing:

There's a land that is brighter than day, and by faith we can see it afar,
For my father waits over the way, to prepare us a dwelling place there,
In the sweet by and by, we shall meet on that beautiful shore...

Mama used to sing that hymn, and I always thought of her in church with us when I heard it.

Now, we kids didn't always make it to church when Daddy was gone. We were lazy. But it always felt right to be in church even when I couldn't concentrate on the sermon.

"Ready?" Daddy called from the porch.

"Ready!" we said in unison, all trying to get out of the door at once.

"Where's the car?" Dewey asked.

"It's parked in the back where we left it," Daddy said. "We're going to walk to church."

"Why?" Nola whined. "My legs hurt."

"Because, my dear, we don't want to be show-offs. People might think we have a love of modern things more than a love for God and His creation," Daddy said.

"But Daddy," Dewey began to whine, "It wouldn't be bragging."

"Let's don't be show-offs," Daddy said.

With that we got our pot of beans and started walking down the road. People were already going into the sanctuary of the Pine

Bluff Presbyterian Church so Nola and I skipped on ahead to find Kit. This was our regular church, but we didn't go like we should.

"Guess what?" I whispered to Kit. "Daddy got us a Model T."

Her eyes widened, and she sucked in her breath. "Is it outside?"

"No," I said, "we hid it behind our house so no one would know about it."

"Why is it a secret?" she said.

"Daddy said we can't be show-offs," I said.

"Well, I'd be showing it," she said as we went to get seated.

Our family filled up one long pew. Aunt Leah wasn't there; Uncle Josh whispered to Daddy that she had gotten sick frying bacon and had to lie down. Kit squeezed in by me.

The preacher walked up to the pulpit. "Today we're serving dinner on the grounds," he said. "If it's too cold, we'll bring the food back inside and make do. I want to encourage everyone, especially our guests, to join us in fellowship."

"When are we gonna sing?" Nola whispered loudly.

"Shhhhh!" I said.

Daddy gave us both the look.

I liked the preacher's voice and tried hard to be still. But he kept going off in so many directions I lost my concentration. Then an elderly grandpa in front of me snorted loudly and breathed out a bubbly, long breath. His head dropped to his chest, and he caught his breath and snored again. I held my breath to keep from laughing until my shoulders shook; that started Nola giggling uncontrollably, and Kit laughed out loud. Daddy reached over to me with the look and pointed to a note he'd written. It said, "This is the Lord's house—treat it with reverence."

I sobered up and wiped my nose with a hanky, but I couldn't look at the girls. Everything was fine until the old gentleman woke up and didn't recognize his whereabouts. He breathed a gurgle through his large nose and looked around, confused. I put my face into my handkerchief to keep from exploding, and Daddy took my elbow rather forcefully. Luckily the sermon ended and everyone stood up to sing the song of invitation just as Daddy was ready to march me out of the church.

When we got up to sing, I saw Miss Bonner and the Terrill family with baby Daniel, and I waved to them. I had shameful thoughts when I saw Mrs. Terrill. I didn't like the way she hogged Daniel and acted like he was hers, and I wanted her to see our new shiny car so she wouldn't feel sorry for us anymore.

At dinner the church ladies put out table-cloths on long tables and heaped food on them. The fried chicken caught my eye, but there was also ham, pork chops, and beef roast. I didn't pay attention to the vegetables; I just wanted meat and dessert. I noticed McKinley was talking with his friends from school as Dewey chased some girls with an imaginary frog.

"Dewey, Daddy's gonna give you more than his look if you don't settle down," I yelled. But he kept on, because Dewey didn't like to eat. I don't know where his flesh and blood came from, because the only things he would eat were biscuits and butter and desserts.

Kit and I walked over to where Miss Bonner stood. She asked if we'd enjoyed the service, and we nodded yes. She asked me if I was glad my daddy was home, and I said, "Oh, yes ma'am."

Then Mrs. Terrill came with Daniel, and he wanted me more than he wanted Mrs. Terrill. He jounced around until she finely gave in and put him on the ground. He went for a table-cloth first, and I caught him before he pulled the plate of fried chicken off. No doubt he was a miniature Dewey!

Daddy came over and picked him up. "How's my boy?" he said to him, and Daniel rocked back and forth trying to get back on the ground so he could pull the tablecloth again. Daddy put him gently down, took each hand, and walked him around until he plopped right on the ground.

Kit and I played peekaboo with him, but he got disinterested in a hurry. He liked moving and pulling things and ended up getting under one of the tables. Nola went in after him, and he was eating dirt. From then on, Daddy held him.

"Daniel has a lot of energy, doesn't he?" Miss Bonner said.

"He's all boy—that's for sure," Daddy said.

"I notice he's developing quickly. He's going to walk early for his age, Mr. Smith," she said. "I watch his progress every day."

"Yes, I understand you're boarding with the Terrills," Daddy said. "By the way, just call me Jim."

"Then Jim it is." She smiled. "It's a very agreeable situation," she continued. "I enjoy the Terrills very much and I have a private room to do my lesson preparation."

Miss Bonner had worn her church dress, made of ruffles and lace, which was much nicer than what she wore to school. I noticed she had pinched her cheeks for color, and when she talked to Daddy, her whole face got pink like she was embarrassed or something.

Daddy handed Daniel to me and said he'd fix us all plates. I thought that was nice of Daddy until Daniel became a wiggly worm. I figured then that Daddy had taken the easiest job. He asked Miss Bonner and the Terrills to join us eating and we all worked at keeping Daniel from squirming. We ate bites in between wiggles.

I looked at people sitting on the steps and on quilts on the ground and at the children, especially boys, running here and there. Even though it was December it wasn't cold or windy, and I dubbed it a day made for the angels. I wondered if Mama could see us from heaven.

After dinner the singing started, and Daddy held a songbook with Miss Bonner. He smiled down at her when Daniel tried to tear a page out. She smiled too.

Dewey was eager to go home to investigate the new automobile again. This encouraged Daddy to break away from the church folks and start walking with us. I turned around to wave good-bye to Daniel and saw Miss Bonner watching us walk away. Daddy turned around about that time and walked back over to her. They talked quietly for a minute and then laughed. Daddy seemed happy to have a new friend.

CHAPTER 13

CHRISTMAS TIME

At dark Daddy lit all the kerosene lamps in the house. He said he needed some light on the subject, because he wanted to check all our lessons. He tapped the tobacco out of his pipe and put some new in. I could see the rings of his pipe smoke in the air, and it had Daddy smells in it.

When Daddy was away, McKinley was a hard task-maker because Daddy had put the fear of the good Lord in him about our lessons. Every day when we came home from school, McKinley made us sit on the porch and do our work. He checked it like an old mother hen and went over it with a fine-toothed comb. We wanted to be lazy, but Daddy had made a bargain with McKinley. If he would make us all good students, Daddy would give him fifty cents a week. If Daddy was gone two or three weeks, McKinley had a good wage.

"Let me see your lessons first, McKinley," Daddy said. "Ummm hmmm, you're coming right along. Good work."

Then he looked at Dewey's and complimented him on his ciphering.

"It's arithmetic, not ciphering, Daddy," Dewey said.

"Ciphering is what I call it, young man; you can call it what you want."

Dewey was fidgeting, wanting to get back in motion. He had begun experimenting with new medicines he claimed he was inventing and had smelly concoctions all over the house. He used everything from kerosene to castor oil mixed with salt, sugar and flour to produce heaven knew what. He didn't say if he meant to have people take them internally or spread them over the skin like vapor rub. Daddy finally told him to get back to his projects but to leave his inventions outdoors so we wouldn't have to smell them.

My work came last. He told me he was proud of my reading, but I needed to work harder on my ciphering. I told him I tried, but it didn't go into my head very fast. He hugged me real close.

"Sister, you can get it if you study hard. If you'll promise to work at it more," he whispered, "tomorrow we'll get a Christmas tree and trim it."

"Yippee!" I yelled, not hesitating. "I promise!"

Sure enough, Daddy took us to the country and cut down a pine tree that would just fit in our parlor. He popped popcorn and we threaded it on string, making ropes to go around and around the tree. Nola and I took strands of Mama's old lace and draped them around it too. When we finished, Daddy said it was the prettiest tree we'd ever had because we did it all by ourselves. He didn't mention he wished Mama could see it, but I figured he was thinking about it.

I was happy Daddy didn't have to go to work until after the first of the year. Later he told me his company had given him a special privilege because his children were alone.

After school every day, Daddy taught the boys how to operate the automobile. Dewey named it Her Majesty, and we all began calling her that, even Daddy. McKinley was a good driver and took it up with caution. Dewey, who had to sit on a pillow, took it up with abandon and squeezed on Daddy's temper from time to time. Some day, not many years from now, drivers would have to get a license to drive a car, but not yet in Arkansas.

Nola and I were both excited about Santa Claus coming to see us. On Christmas Eve we had neighbors stop by with Christmas wishes. Nola and I, mostly I, made batches of black walnut fudge, which we wrapped in paper. Daddy took us in Her Majesty to our friends' houses in the afternoon to deliver the candy. The last stop was the Terrills.

"Oh, you sweet things. That looks delicious," Mrs. Terrill said. "Come on in and have some hot chocolate."

"Where's Allibeth?" Daddy asked, calling Miss Bonner by her given name.

"Went to Louisiana to be with her family for Christmas. She'll be back after the first of the year."

I could tell Daddy was disappointed, and I was too.

"Where's the baby?" I asked.

"Been sleeping for about an hour," Mrs. Terrill said.

"Could I talk to you privately?" Daddy asked her.

"Come on in the kitchen, and we'll talk while I get the hot chocolate ready, and you can have some coffee with Mr. Terrill," she said. It struck me odd that some wives called their husbands Mister, but Daddy told me it was being respectful if that's what a wife wanted to do.

Soon they brought us our hot chocolate and went back to the kitchen. Daddy and the Terrills talked for a long while, and Dewey itched to get back in the car. When they came out, Daddy looked very solemn, and Mrs. Terrill looked pleased.

"I want you to know we'll be moving to Oklahoma soon," Mrs. Terrill announced.

"Wow!" I said. "When are you leaving?"

"Right after Christmas," she said. "My parents live in Tulsa, and Mr. Terrill wants to work in the oil fields. People are making fortunes in that part of the country."

"Hmmm," Nola said, "that means we get our baby back."

Daddy rushed over to us. "Time to go, girls," he said. "Old Santa will be out and about before you can say Jack Johnson."

"But we haven't even gotten to see Daniel, and it's Christmas," Nola whined.

"The little fellow needs his rest," Daddy said. "Let's go get you in bed so Santa Claus can come."

Before I fell asleep, I heard sleigh bells, so I knew Santa Claus really was going to find us. His bells sounded a lot like cowbells, but this was Arkansas.

I squeezed my eyes shut and asked God to protect Santa Claus from harm. I asked Him to remind Mama that it was Christmas and to look down on our pretty tree.

Soon Nola began to shake me, and I couldn't wake up. Finally, she punched on my arm, and I bounced up.

"Ella! It's Christmas!" she yelled. I thought I'd just fallen asleep.

I shivered from excitement. Then, Nola and I pulled on our dresses and ran to the parlor. I didn't expect much. There had been times when Santa had left us only fruit and nuts. But this year he knew we had high hopes. Maybe he knew we'd lost our mama and needed it to be special.

Nola opened her present, and it was a china doll. She touched her shiny face and declared she was Bette Jean.

"Where in thunder did you think up that name?" Dewey asked.

"None of your beeswax," Nola said. "It's my doll and my choice."

My present was a gold cross on a chain. I asked Daddy to put it around my neck and hugged him big because I knew he must have told Santa I wanted one.

Santa had brought Dewey a pearl-handled pocketknife and McKinley a pocket watch. They were so happy, but I couldn't see why. A knife or a clock didn't seem like presents to me.

The long, wool stockings we'd tacked to the fireplace were full. Fruit and hard Christmas candy peeped out of the tops.

"What did Santa get you, Daddy?" Nola asked.

"The looks on your faces," he said and smiled a million-dollar smile.

"Here's something from us, Daddy," McKinley said and handed him his present. "Dew and I earned some money helping Aunt Leah, and the girls have a little something for you too."

Daddy opened up a book called *Our American Heritage* and then our package of special black walnut fudge that we'd—mostly I'd—made.

"You children! What am I gonna do with you?" He hugged each of us with an "umh umh umph!"

"Now, what's that big package no one opened?" Daddy said.

"Whose is it?" Dew asked, jumping around.

"Look at the tag, and see who it's for," Daddy said.

Dewey beat us all to it and yelled out, "It's for everyone here!"

We rushed over and began tearing at the paper. It was a Victrola phonograph machine built into a cabinet! I thought it would have a little horn on it to make the music travel out into the room and a wind-up handle. But according to Daddy, the sound-reproducing horn was built inside the rather small cabinet. Santa brought two seventy-eight records for us to play. One was "In the Good Old Summertime" and the other was "Take Me Out to the Ball Game."

They were summer songs, but we were happy as larks to play them over and over. Dewey kept opening up the Victrola and pulling the records out to see how it worked, and Daddy finally blew his stack.

"Santa Claus goes to all this trouble, and you're going to ruin this Victrola and the records! Now, be gentle with it!"

It took some practice with it, but we finally mastered our impatience. We played those two songs all afternoon.

"We'll go to Little Rock one of these days and get some more records," Daddy said, looking pleased.

"This is so exciting!" Nola said. "Now, the boys don't have to play music!"

Daddy laughed. "Sweetheart, one of these days we'll buy a record that says McKinley and Dewey Smith on it."

"Did you rob a bank, Daddy, or did we get rich?" Dewey asked.

Daddy laughed again. "No, the Cotton Belt Railroad people gave me a raise."

When Nola finally got bored with music, I went with her into our room. She played with her doll on the bed, putting her under the cover and telling her what to do.

I stood in front of the mirror, turning myself one way and then the other, admiring my shiny new necklace. Then I pinched my cheeks to look healthy.

"You're primping, Ella," Nola said. "The preacher said that's vanity."

"Not either," I said and turned away from the mirror. "At least I got something I can take with me all the time instead of a silly old doll."

"I'm telling Daddy," Nola said.

"Let's just play dress-up," I said. "You can be a mama, and I'll be a fancy singer."

"I'll be a fancy mama then," said Nola, and she put on one of the little hats Mama had gotten her when she was smaller. I was about to insult her when Daddy came in.

"It's about time to go to Leah's for Christmas dinner. You girls going to help pick up the house?" he said.

"Sure," we both said. We were cooperative in getting the house straight because we were looking forward to the feast.

"You're the best daddy in the world," I said, thinking about our morning.

"You're the best children," he said. "Now, let's go eat Christmas dinner."

Aunt Leah made turkey and dressing for Uncle Josh because that was his favorite food. She said her stomach was queasy, and she couldn't eat anything she cooked. I looked at the sweet potato pie and chocolate cake and wondered how she could turn them down. We stayed there the rest of the day playing games and going back to the table to nibble again. We didn't get to see Daniel all day, but Daddy said he knew for sure Santa Claus had visited him.

We sat around taking turns leading a song while Aunt Leah played carols, and Daddy strummed his guitar. It was a beautiful sunny day. We were so lucky to be in the part of Arkansas where the weather was mostly good, even in the winter.

Back home that night Daddy fell asleep sitting up in the old green armchair.

"Let's hit the sack," Dewey said, very unlike himself. He convinced Daddy to go on to bed. But he and McKinley stayed up talking in the parlor.

I slipped out of bed and into the parlor to see why they weren't asleep.

"What are you two plotting?" I asked.

"Just talking about Daniel," Dewey said.

"What about Daniel?"

"Sister, don't get upset, because I'm not sure I heard right," McKinley whispered to me. "But I think I heard Daddy tell Aunt Leah that Mrs. Terrill wants to adopt Daniel."

"She can't," I said, beginning to tune up and cry. "He's ours."

"Daddy said he can't take care of him, and Aunt Leah's not able to now."

"Daddy can't just give him away," I said. "I'll ask him. I bet you heard wrong."

"Don't go asking Daddy about this because he'll think I was eavesdropping," McKinley said.

"Daniel is ours, not anybody else's! And if Mrs. Terrill thinks she's taking him off to Oklahoma, she's got another think coming."

"Go get in bed now, Sister," McKinley said. "Things will work out like God wants them to work out."

Soon I heard the boys go to their room. Dewey tossed and turned and talked in his sleep most of the night. McKinley didn't settle in early either. I heard the whistle of a train in the distance, and I was glad Daddy wasn't on it. I could find out about Daniel in the morning.

CHAPTER 14

A NEW BABY

Daddy woke us up the next morning for pancakes and sorghum molasses. Oh, how I hated that syrup. Even the smell of it reminded me of being sick. Mama used to give me castor oil flavored with sorghum. This was my parents' favorite medicine because they thought it got rid of bad colds and stomachaches and other pain, real or imagined.

Daddy was quiet. "What're you thinking about, Daddy?" Nola asked.

"I've got the day-after-Christmas blues, Nola," he said.

The boys brought the bucket of milk in. Daddy looked at it and said Pokey was still giving us a good amount. I thought if Pokey could talk, she could tell Daddy about a lot of things. Dewey would be in a heap of trouble for always squirting the cat, and we would all be in trouble for not keeping the cow lot clean.

Dewey wasn't his cheerful self this morning. He sat down quietly and ate his pancakes, because they were one of the three foods he enjoyed eating. McKinley asked Daddy if they could have a talk after a while. Daddy nodded yes.

Suddenly someone was banging on our kitchen door. Dewey was the first to hop up. He opened it wide, and Kit ran in screaming.

"Now catch your breath, honey," Daddy said. "What's the matter?"

"Daddy says will you go get the doctor?" Kit panted.

"Who's sick?"

"Mama's having the baby," Kit yelled and ran out the door.

"McKinley, you and Dewey get in the wagon and go ask Mrs. Harlen and Mrs. Terrill to come to Aunt Leah's. I'll take the car and find Dr. Jordan," Daddy said.

"Ella, you and Nola just stay put until you hear from me," he said, hurrying out the back door.

My heart pounded in my ears. Not many months ago, Mama had had little Daniel, and it had killed her.

"Please, God, don't take Aunt Leah from us too," I whispered.

We sat and waited. Nola had never been so quiet, and I couldn't even bear to pick up a book to read so I hummed a hymn that Nola liked called, "At the Cross." It seemed to soothe her; I know it did me.

Soon McKinley and Dewey rode up in front of Aunt Leah's house with Mrs. Harlen, who climbed out of the wagon taking her apron off. Shortly thereafter, Daddy and Dr. Jordan drove up.

Uncle Josh let them in, and we all bundled up and waited on our porch for some news.

Finally Dr. Jordan came out wiping his face with a handkerchief. He and Daddy talked for a minute, and then Daddy stood up.

"No baby yet!" he yelled. Then he walked over to us.

"This may take a while," he said.

"I need to talk to you, Daddy," Dew shouted as he came from out back.

"Sure, Son. Is something wrong?"

"Don't know. Just need to talk to you," Dewey said.

They went into the kitchen and closed the door.

What were all the secrets? I was curious, yet I was worried about Aunt Leah more. I wished I could talk to Kit, but she was in their house.

Aunt Leah didn't have that baby until four o'clock the next morning. It was a little baby girl named Rebeccah after my mother. Kit had guessed right about her baby being a girl.

Dr. Jordan said she had good lungs because she was a mighty good yeller. Kit and I hugged.

"Dr. Jordan said Mama made it fine," Kit said.

"Good," I said. "I'll bet the baby's cute."

"She's chubby and even has hair," Kit said. "Come over to see her."

"I'll have to ask Daddy if I can," I said and started in the house. I really wanted to see my aunt doing all right with my own eyes.

But Daddy wouldn't allow us to go back to Aunt Leah's. He said there was too much traffic in her house. I sure needed to talk to my best friend some more, but that was out. I tried to not think about Daniel.

That afternoon I finally got the courage to talk to Daddy. I was always afraid he'd get mad if I asked the wrong questions.

"Daddy, are you giving Daniel to Mrs. Terrill?" I asked.

Dewey's eyes popped open bigger than half dollars. McKinley cleared his throat. Nola looked down at her shoes. Then Daddy spoke.

"Sister, here's the way this thing with the Terrills is going to work. Mrs. Terrill is taking Daniel with her on the train to Tulsa. She will stay with her parents until Mr. Terrill follows with their furniture. In the meantime she has agreed to care for Daniel until I can make other arrangements for him in Pine Bluff."

Relief went all over me. Daniel would be safe. We would get him back.

"What else are you wondering about?" Daddy said.

"Aunt Leah. Is it for sure she's going to live?" I knew she had lost at least two infants at birth. They were Kit's younger brothers.

"Aunt Leah is fine," he said. "Don't you worry about things like that, Ella."

"Come on, Sister," Nola said. "Let's go play dolls."

I got up and put my dishes in the dishpan.

"Whew! I feel better, Daddy," I said and went off to play.

Nola and I played dolls a long while. I cut out a dress for my last year's doll and tried to sew it together. Nola didn't want one for her doll. She said mine looked like I'd sewed up a rag.

Daddy came in the nick of time to save an argument.

"Want to go for a ride in Her Majesty?" he asked.

"Why not?" I said, just like the boys did sometimes.

Daddy cranked up Her Majesty and took us for a ride down Main Street. When we reached the Terrills' house, Daddy stopped. Mrs. Terrill came out with Daniel.

"I'd like to take him home until you leave," Daddy said.

"Oh, I can't let him go," Mrs. Terrill said. "It'll get him too mixed up."

I thought Mrs. Terrill was the one mixed up. He was our baby.

"When are you planning on leaving?" Daddy asked.

"Tomorrow morning," she said.

Daddy had a stern look on his face. "Tell you what, Mrs. Terrill—we'll keep him tonight and meet you at the station in the morning."

Mrs. Terrill didn't look any too happy. Daddy left her no choice though, so she handed me the baby's sleepwear and diapers. She looked worried as we left.

But we made the most of having Daniel and entertained him royally. Daddy even played his guitar for Daniel, and the boys joined him with their instruments.

"Dance pretty," Nola told Daniel, and he performed for us.

He held on to a chair and bounced up and down. Then he turned around and grinned and plopped onto the floor. I picked him up and hugged him, but he squirmed and wanted the floor again. Daddy laughed, and the boys took turns letting him pick at their instrument strings.

I tried to brush his pretty red curls at bedtime, but he screamed and grabbed the comb and chewed on it hungrily.

"Want to sleep with Nola and me?" I cooed to him.

"Sister," Daddy said, "let me just take him in my room. I think he'll sleep better in there."

We all went to sleep and didn't hear a peep out of Daniel because he was all danced out.

"Nola," I said in our room. "Aren't you excited to start to school next month?"

"No! I don't want to go to school!" she said.

"You can't stay by yourself," I said. "Aunt Leah will be busy with the baby."

Then I started telling her how much fun it was at recess, which got her excited. I decided I would mention this to Daddy in the morning. But before morning came, Daniel woke everybody up in the house, crying loudly and mournfully. Daddy walked him around for a while, but nothing would make him stop. When I went into the parlor, Daddy was getting him ready to leave.

"He wants his mama," Daddy said. "He thinks of Mrs. Terrill as Mama."

It didn't seem right to me, so I held out my hands to Daniel. He turned from me, wrestled in Daddy's arms, and screamed bloody murder. Maybe he did want Mrs. Terrill after all.

Daddy got McKinley up, and they took my little brother back to the Terrills. By the time they returned home, we were ready to go see Daniel off at the station,

Kit came over to go with us, so Her Majesty was loaded to the gills. Mr. Terrill took Daniel and Mrs. Terrill to the train station in their wagon. Nola and I held our hands out to Daniel but he turned away from us. He wanted Mrs. Terrill, not us. Daddy and the boys stood at the side of the Terrill wagon watching the sad goodbye with blank faces. Mr. Terrill carried the suitcases up the steps of the train and stored them for Mrs. Terrill. She got on the train and put Daniel in the window so we could see him leave. We never did get to hug him one last time. I blew him a kiss and the train squealed off into the morning. I held Nola's hand and we both cried.

I had a sinking feeling about Mrs. Terrill taking Daniel off with her. Would we ever see our baby again? He was the last person my mama had loved, and I didn't want to lose that part of her.

CHAPTER 15

LEARNING LIFE LESSONS

I remember when Daddy decided to teach us about practical things. Good weather inspired Daddy to give our place a thorough general cleaning. He had the boys rake leaves and clean up the yard while Nola and I scrubbed the kitchen. Daddy cleaned the cow lot out himself and gave the boys a good scolding for letting things go.

After all of that was done, we gathered up all our dirty clothes. We separated the whites from the coloreds. Then the boys hauled water from Aunt Leah's well and filled the black kettle out back and lit a fire under it. When it got to boiling, I added lye soap. First we put all the white clothes in. Daddy took a paddle and sloshed them around until the dirt came out. Then he pulled them out with the paddle and put them in a basket. We didn't wash our clothes as Aunt Leah did on a rub board.

Next he put the dark clothes in and boiled and worked them around. After this was done, he poured out the hot water, placed cold water inside the kettle, and removed it from the fire. He rinsed the white clothes first and then the coloreds. Then we all joined in wringing the water out of them and hung them to dry on two clotheslines for the day. When it was time, we gathered them all in to fold and put away. I say folded, but we wadded most of the clothes up and stuffed them into drawers. Still, they smelled like sunshine.

We took more care with our good clothing that we wore only on special occasions. Daddy showed me how Mama had sprinkled the clothes with water so she could iron them. We rolled the moist clothes tightly, put them in a basket, and left them overnight. The next day I would get my first lesson in ironing.

We had two heavy irons we heated on top of the cook stove. Daddy pulled a hot one off and wrapped a thick cloth around the handle. He showed me how to hold it and how to press the wrinkles out of clothes.

I wanted to get it over fast. When he wasn't looking, I tried to hurry and pulled the iron back too quickly. Unfortunately, I branded myself in the middle of my stomach, right where the skin peeked out of my blouse at the bottom where two buttons were missing. It hurt, but I didn't dare make a fuss. It was my fault, and I owned up to it. Daddy put some chlorine salve on the burn and told me I didn't have to iron anymore that day, but my career wasn't quite over. That was one of my jobs from then on, and I never tried to hurry again. I was a quick learner when it came to mistakes. I was branded forever on my midsection to remind me lest I forget.

Daddy doctored my injury with chlorine salve again before bedtime, and Nola and I got into our nightgowns. Daddy said quietly he would be going back to work tomorrow. Then the next tomorrow we would start back to school.

Nola started crying, and I was quiet, real quiet.

"Would you like me to play you some music to get you to sleep?" he asked.

"Okay," I said as pitifully as I could.

He sat down by our bed with his guitar and began strumming. He sang softly in his tender voice, and I thought he sounded like an angel. "Sleep, baby, sleep, close your bright eyes. Listen to your daddy, while he sings lullabies…" I couldn't help but sing along softly so as not to cry. Our voices blended in sweet harmony and it was a moment to be treasured.

Nola began to sob quietly, as she always did when Daddy sang with melancholy a song which he must have heard in his parents' home as a child himself. I tickled her back real softly and she tried to hide as she slipped her thumb in her mouth. She went fast asleep, but Daddy was still singing as I drifted away. I was too tired to fight sleep or to think about tomorrow or the next tomorrow.

In the morning Daddy took us for one more ride. Aunt Leah agreed to let Kit go with us.

Daddy laid down some rules about the car. Her Majesty was to stay put with its tarp on until he returned. If anyone went to town, it was to be in the wagon. The law would catch up with us if we disobeyed. Now, I knew if Dewey could get Her Majesty started by himself and get his pillow situated right, he might break his promise. But I felt certain that was impossible.

We rode into the country a piece. The pine trees were so tall they wouldn't let the sun see us.

On the way back home, we stopped by Miss Bonner's. Mr. Terrill was loading his wagon for Tulsa, but he said he was leaving Miss Bonner enough furniture to get by.

Daddy asked Miss Bonner to take a ride with us. I couldn't see how we would all fit in the car, but we managed. Daddy drove faster than usual and turned a corner rapidly to impress Miss Bonner, but it scared us. Miss Bonner held her composure, but we three girls screamed.

Miss Bonner offered to stop by to check on us after Daddy left for work. I thought that was a good thing and a bad thing. How in tarnation would we be able to be our usual lazy selves with somebody watching us?

After we dropped Miss Bonner at her house, we stopped by Aunt Leah's. Daddy hadn't allowed us to see the baby but once. Aunt Leah didn't want her to get germs.

My aunt still had another week of bed rest because having little Rebeccah must have made her real tired. Kit and Uncle Josh were doing the cooking. I asked Aunt Leah how they were doing. She made a face behind Kit's back, but I was on Kit's side. She hadn't been taught to cook because Aunt Leah wouldn't allow her in the kitchen.

Aunt Leah was cranky about the baby and didn't want anyone to hold her. I didn't want to hold her anyway because she reminded me too much of Daniel. I looked at her closely, and saw Uncle Josh in her face. She had more hair than I'd ever seen on a baby. With the sun shining on her head, it looked like strained honey. Aunt Leah didn't call her by my mama's full name. She called her Becca.

After we visited, Daddy took us home. He went to Dalby's Grocery to stock us up with groceries before he left for the railroad, and late in the afternoon he walked down to the train station. We all stood on the porch and watched him until he was almost out of sight. Unlike Kit, I didn't believe it was bad luck to watch him go. He turned and gave us a little salute, and Nola and I blew him a kiss.

"Let's make some music," McKinley said, and turned to lead us into the house.

Dewey pulled out the fiddle, McKinley began stamping his foot in time, and they played "Arkansas Traveler." That music just about saved my tender heart during times like that.

I looked at McKinley and knew he was trying to get our minds off being lonely.

"McKinley," I said, "you're a real prince."

He wouldn't look up. I didn't know at the time that he was thinking about getting enough age on him to join the army and help fight in the war. He just kept on playing and patting his foot in time.

CHAPTER 16

TROY CLARK

The years rolled by swiftly, and the children in our family accepted its circumstances of staying alone when Daddy worked. Nola adapted well to school and liked learning new things. She even learned to milk! I was growing up a step at a time, trying to grow into my true self. I missed Daniel, but my memories of him began to fade as I turned my mind more and more toward music and doing my part in the daily rituals of life. I loved the boys including me when they made music and they seemed to get a kick out of my making up lyrics to a song.

Everything was going our way until to my great surprise and shock McKinley announced he would enlist in the army when he turned eighteen in January. He would head to Fort Pike and leave us all behind. Dew acted brave but he took the news hard. We had to get ourselves together so that we would be happy with what we had.

That summer Aunt Leah taught Kit and me how to crochet. I didn't do a perfect job at it, but it was fun. I even took my crochet satchel with me when we went fishing. It filled time making hot pads and doilies when the fish weren't biting.

McKinley got tired of being in charge of us. He wished so badly we lived inside the town of Pine Bluff so he could play for the high school Zebras. They were national champions, and McKinley just knew he could make the team. But we were simply too far away and had to continue with our one-room-school learning.

We didn't see him much around the house anymore as he was either tossing the football back and forth with a friend or going off with the gang, as he liked to say. The one thing he didn't give up at the house was his music and that helped us all.

One fellow musician was a boy named Troy Clark who'd lost his mother the winter before to pneumonia. Troy was like us—almost an orphan, except for a father who was bringing him up all alone. He came over most every day after school and helped McKinley shine the car. They looked at the engine and the radiator and tested the horn. Then they got Dewey and played music on the porch until sundown.

"I'd like to take that automobile apart and see what makes it tick," Troy said to McKinley.

"Yep, we'll get under it one day and see what its guts are made of," McKinley said, pulling out his guitar. Troy picked up his own guitar, and they broke into "Under the Double Eagle."

I watched the two of them playing their instruments. They were so different, but both of them had a string of girlfriends. McKinley was tall, lanky, and athletic, and Troy was shorter with muscles on his arms from throwing balls and doing hard work.

"Mack, did you know 'Under the Double Eagle' is an Austrian march?" Troy said.

"No kidding," McKinley said. "A march?"

"Yeah, some guy wrote it to honor the Austrian coat of arms," Troy said.

That just about did it for me. Troy Clark was not only charming and musical, but he was smart too. I thought he and my brother were about the handsomest boys I knew. I was proud McKinley was kin to me and decided then that I would have to marry Troy when I got old enough. I would sing with the band and be a fairy princess wife, and I would definitely never cook again because Troy would be rich enough to have me a maid and a butler.

One evening in late autumn, the wind started up and began to blow the trees back and forth.

"Is it gonna come a storm?" Nola asked.

"Supposed to come a norther tonight," McKinley said as the day darkened quickly into night. "Make sure you have enough covers for your beds."

"What's a norther?" asked Nola.

"Some cold, bad weather," he said. "Time for bed. Daddy said to get you two in bed earlier on school nights."

Silence filled the house as we prepared for bed. As I got in beside Nola, I heard the sound of light rain like small tinkle bells. A train whistle sang out in the background, and a gust of strong wind overturned something in the yard. The norther was here.

Early the next morning, Dewey woke Nola. "You need to help me milk this morning, Nola. McKinley had to go to school early today."

"I don't want to," she said. "It's too cold!"

"I don't like to milk either," he said. "But we need the milk."

"But I don't want to milk! And why can't Ella do it? I'm little," she said in her smallest, most pitiful voice.

"Because Sister is taking care of the kitchen!" Dewey said.

"It's not fair!"

"Yes, it is."

"No, it's not!"

"Oh, you all just get your clothes on, and let's go!" I yelled.

I could see Pokey wasn't going to get milked this morning. I picked up my books and walked out the door. I knew this was going to be a long argument.

"The biscuits are on the stove. See you at school!" I yelled, pulling on a sweater.

I wasn't expecting to see the weather so different. It had sleeted a fine, thin coat of glass over everything in sight. My nose was freezing! I slipped and slid for about ten minutes but didn't get very far.

I went back for my coat, just as Dewey was wrapping his biscuits in a handkerchief.

"Are you okay?" he asked.

"No, it's freezing…" I chattered. Then I grabbed Nola's hand and helped her with her coat, and the three of us went by Aunt Leah's. Uncle Josh came to the door.

"Kit got sick in the night. Tell Miss Bonner she won't be in school today," he said.

"We'll bring her lessons to her!" Dewey yelled.

The wind was blowing strong and cold. Dewey and I got on each side of Nola to keep the blustery weather away from her. By the time we reached the schoolhouse, icy rain was pouring down.

The boys kept feeding the fire for Miss Bonner, but the only ones who felt the warmth were sitting by the stove. Ice began to form around the windows, and cold air whistled through the cracks in the building. At noon Miss Bonner dismissed school.

"Practice your lessons, children. Going home doesn't mean going home to play."

We all said yes ma'am and went out the door. McKinley and Dewey ran ahead of us to start a fire. Nola and I tried to run to get out of the icy rain, but the wind kept pushing us back. By the time we got to our porch, we were both soaked. We changed clothes and put our shoes by the fire.

Nola talked in a raspy voice.

"Are you all right?" I asked.

"My throat is getting sore," she said.

I got the Vicks salve out and put some on her neck with a warm cloth over it. It was smelly, like strong mint or worse, but it somehow soothed Nola. She felt hot to the touch.

When she began to shake with chills, I got scared.

"Dewey, will you go tell Uncle Josh Nola's sick?"

Dewey ran out the door in a flash. Soon Uncle Josh came over.

"Looks like Nola and Kit have the same thing," he said. "I think it's the flu."

Up to this point, none of us had been sick. I'm sure I'd had fever before, but I didn't remember it. Nola cried softly.

"My head hurts!" she said and writhed from side to side.

Uncle Josh told us to keep her in bed. He would ask Aunt Leah what he gave Kit to make her feel better.

"I'll be back after a while," he said. "Keep her warm."

I tucked Nola in and piled quilts on her. She was shaking, and she was still burning up with fever. I looked to Dewey for help because he had wanted to be a doctor for as long as I could remember. He still experimented and made some awful concoctions in the name of science but none fit for a sick person.

"We need to rub her down with alcohol," he said. "That'll get the fever down."

We looked everywhere but didn't have any. We decided to just try and get her to sleep. We loaded more quilts on her because Dewey had read that a person could sweat off a fever. She finally slept, but she was fitful. By that time it was dark.

McKinley took Nola's illness very lightly. He thought we were in a panic for nothing.

"She'll be all right by the morning," he said, lighting a lamp in our room. "Don't get excited."

Dewey ignored him. "I wish we had one of those new telephones," he said thoughtfully. "I'd call the doctor."

I stared at him. "Dewey, he'd have to have one too."

"That's what I mean, Sister. If we both had a telephone, we wouldn't have to go to kingdom come for help when we need it. You wait and see. Everybody will have a telephone someday."

Dewey didn't make sense sometimes. Telephones would never be a common thing. I remembered Dewey telling Mrs. Harlen that he'd learned about electricity and the telephone at school. She had said she didn't believe in that old science stuff. So, I took her at her word. After all, she was a grown-up.

I had never felt so cold. It was lucky McKinley had gathered wood this morning. But it was night, and we had to let fire die out in the fireplace. Dewey and I made pallets on the floor at each side of Nola's bed. We kept piling on the blankets and still weren't warm. Nola began to cough, loud croupy coughs. I shivered and said my prayers.

Uncle Josh came over to check on Nola just as we got settled. When he gave her medicine for her cough, she threw up. But, it seemed to relieve her, and she settled down.

"Uncle Josh, we'll be all right now. You probably need to see about Kit, don't you?" Dewey asked.

"Son, I hate to leave you, but I think you're right. I put some broth on the stove for when Nola wakes up. Just try to go to sleep, and when the dawn comes, we'll get you some help."

He went out the door, and the freezing gust of wind sent a shock through the house. We tried to sleep after he left, but we all tossed and turned. When the gray dawn came, everything was white outside. The wind was still howling through the cracks in the walls. I was glad Pokey was safe in the barn and Her Majesty was covered up.

When McKinley woke up the next morning, he was stunned at Nola's condition. She moaned as her fever raged, and Mama's death came back to all of us as Nola struggled for breath.

CHAPTER 17

SPREADING ILLNESS

Dewey went to Aunt Leah's. Uncle Josh came back with him and decided to get the wagon ready to go after Dr. Jordan. Nola ached all over, so I wet a cloth and dabbed it on her face. It made her so angry she got out of bed and lay down on my pallet. She put her thumb in her mouth and turned on her side like a baby. She would fall asleep, get fitful, and sit straight up, looking around. She was burning up.

Dewey came inside half frostbitten. Uncle Josh had the team ready to go to town.

"Stay with us, Dewey. I'm scared," I said.

"I was planning to, Sister. Uncle Josh is taking McKinley with him."

I made some cornmeal mush for us. I thought I could warm it up for Nola when she woke up. The weather outside had started all over again

"I hope the mule team can keep its footing on that ice," Dewey said.

"I hope they can get back fast—that's all I want," I said.

The grandfather clock ticked away the morning. Finally, it was two o'clock, and Uncle Josh still wasn't back. Neither Nola nor I had touched the cornmeal mush.

Dewey was preoccupied, trying to mix up something with camphor in it for Nola. I eyed it suspiciously and tried to distract him.

"Dew, don't you think you ought to check and see if Uncle Josh made it?" I asked.

He hopped up and put on the rubber boots he wore for milking. Then he put on Daddy's old slicker. It was about the only dry piece of clothing in the house.

I watched Dewey as he crept over to Aunt Leah's, trying not to slip on the ice. He stood at her door a minute or two listening. Then he turned around and started down the road to town.

I wanted so badly to know what Aunt Leah had told him, but I didn't dare leave Nola. Kit must still really be sick too.

It was a dark day. By four o'clock, the kerosene lamps weren't doing much good. I checked to see that there was plenty of wood.

Nola slept on and off, but her fever never broke. Neither Uncle Josh nor the boys were anywhere in sight. I hugged Nola to me and sang to her. It seemed to calm her so I stayed on that path until dark came.

It came, and the fever didn't give up. I kept bathing Nola's face and arms in cold water. She no longer protested. Finally, I pulled her up on the bed and placed several quilts over her. I turned out the lamps and slipped in beside her with my clothes on. If Dewey and the doctor came, I wanted to be dressed for whatever we had to do.

I stayed awake listening. All I heard was freezing rain hitting the house, ping, ping, ping. Nola would sleep a few minutes, and then she'd sit up and say something crazy. I held on to her and closed my eyes for just a minute.

When I opened them, Dewey was standing over me whispering that the doctor had come. Light was beginning to show through the ice-crusted window.

Dr. Jordan lit the lamp and pulled a chair up beside Nola.

"Ella, let's get this cover off her and see what's going on here," he said.

Nola was fitful and woke up seeing a ghost on the wall. She was so hoarse I couldn't understand her words.

She banged her head against the headboard and screamed out. "What's wrong with me?"

"I believe you've got influenza, dearest one," he said and put a thermometer under her tongue.

"Has any blood been in her sputum?" he asked Dewey.

"I don't know about sputum, but she coughed up blood."

Dr. Jordan pulled out his pocket watch and felt Nola's pulse. He didn't say anything.

"What are you going to do for her?" Dewey asked quietly.

"Got to get this fever down right now, Dewey. I'm giving her some aspirin, and she needs lots of fresh water. Then you need to get some broth down her."

"She's not hungry," I said.

"I'll stay with you until she eats. That'll at least be a start in her recovery," the doctor said.

"Uncle Josh brought some broth over, but she couldn't keep it on her stomach," I told Dr. Jordan.

"We'll just have to keep trying to get it down her," he said patiently.

I lit the kerosene lamp and looked at Nola. In the dawn of the early morning, her face had a bluish cast. She began coughing again, and Dr. Jordan had her take the aspirin. Then he went to the kitchen to make up a gargle for her.

"Dewey, this is soda and boric acid," the doctor said. "Make sure Nola doesn't swallow it, but have her gargle three times a day."

"Doc," said Dewey, "somebody told Uncle Josh to make a poultice out of grease and boiled onions for Kit. Will that work for Nola?"

Dr. Jordan snickered.

"Son, I imagine that makes you smell pretty awful, but I don't think it'll cure influenza."

"Where did Nola get this?" Dewey asked.

"Probably in the air, Son," Dr. Jordan said. "Let me show you how to mix this elixir, and you'll know how to make a gargle next time."

Dewey was already getting his first lesson in doctoring.

They both came back into our bedroom, Dr. Jordan with a bottle and Dewey with a spoon. The room was cold and smelled of mildewed clothing and sickness.

"I need to find your daddy," he told Dewey quietly. "Do you know what section he's working right now?"

"No sir," Dewey said, "but Uncle Josh can tell you. Daddy always leaves his whereabouts with him."

The doctor finished up, closed his black bag, and started out. "I'll be back from Leah's in a bit, children," he said. "I'll come back and stay through the night with you. But I have to tell you, this is serious, and I have to reach your daddy."

Dr. Jordan sounded eerily afraid himself. As he walked out, I got down from the bed, and a cold shiver went all over me.

McKinley brought damp firewood in from the porch and put it on the hearth. No sense in trying to get wet firewood started. The icy rain had let up, but the wind still howled.

Nola woke up again and sat up thinking she saw a ghost on the wall again. I felt of her head, and it was blazing hot.

"Dew! McKinley! Nola's burning up!" I screamed. "Get Dr. Jordan back over here!"

Dewey ran to Aunt Leah's and back.

"He's doctoring Kit. He can't get her to wake up," Dewey said, out of breath.

Dr. Jordan ran back and forth from Aunt Leah's to Nola all night. I found him some of Daddy's clothes to wear since his were completely wet. We sat beside Nola until morning broke.

As that day wore on, the weather stopped torturing Pine Bluff so badly. But Nola wasn't better. Her chest moved in and out slowly with a loud, wispy rattle. Dr. Jordan had put Vicks salve on her chest and back to help her breathe. The smell made me dizzy, and my stomach rumbled from not eating.

"How is Kit?" I asked Dr. Jordan.

"We got her through the night, and her fever broke. She should be fine in a few days. She's just weak. Now, we just have to get this young lady better."

Daddy's clothes on Dr. Jordan were baggy and wrinkled from the long night. His usual clean-shaven face was heavy with whiskers.

"I'll bet it's not fun to be a doctor," I said.

"Seeing children sick certainly isn't fun," he said. "But I wouldn't choose anything else to do in this life."

I thought that was a very noble thing to say.

"Doctor, is my daddy coming home?"

"If he gets our message, I know he will, Ella. We sent him a telegraph."

Since Aunt Leah had sent over flour and lard, I asked if I could make gravy and biscuits.

"You do anything you're big enough to do, young lady," he said. "If you cook it, I'll surely eat it."

That's when I learned the busier I get, the better off I am. That way, I can pretend I'm in another place with a lighter set of problems.

McKinley got the fire ready, and I got the bread pan down. Nola was still coughing and wheezing. My mind couldn't think straight, and I did well to make a pan of bread.

Dewey went out to milk, and the bucket was frozen before he got to the cow lot. Somehow, he managed to get some milk for the gravy. After we ate, Dr. Jordan took a bowl in and tried to feed some small biscuit crumbs in gravy to Nola. She was too nauseated to eat.

About noon the fire was blazing in the fireplace, and the ice had about melted around the windows. Nola's fever broke, and the bed was wet as water. Dewey and I got her onto the pallet on the floor and took all the blankets off. We tried to shake the feather mattress out, but it wasn't a job for two small children. Dr. Jordan walked into the room.

"Dewey, can you boys hitch up your team and take me back to my place? We'll either get my wife or Miss Bonner to come over for the night. There's sickness at your Aunt Leah's house, so it wouldn't do much good to take you there."

"But Daddy's coming home, isn't he?"

"Don't know for sure," the doctor said. "Depends on the weather on down the road."

What we didn't know was that all the railroad people had been called off to another site with no communication available.

Daddy had pointed out to us many times that railroad tracks were built high off the ground on packed dirt and gravel. This way water could drain off the tracks. But when a big rain came, the water could still cause a weak spot in the railroad tracks.

Though we wouldn't know until later, a locomotive had turned over in Texas and injured several people. Daddy and other workers were transported there to repair the rails and set the train upright.

We were weary from worrying about Nola, but when we didn't hear from Daddy, we had to make do.

While the boys and Dr. Jordan started off toward town, I remade the bed with what was left of our blankets. Then I warmed some water and washed Nola's face and arms. I tried to brush her hair out, but she started to cry. It hurt her head too badly.

I got out my books and practiced my hateful arithmetic while Nola slept. I drifted off myself, but I awoke to the sound of a wagon out front and saw two figures. I stumbled over to the window to see which of the ladies the boys was bringing with them. It wasn't a lady I saw. Charlie Wright was driving our team of mules, and Dewey was sitting in the back. McKinley was missing.

Dewey hopped out and came in the house.

"Don't say anything, Ella!"

"Why is Charlie with you?"

"Dr. Jordan's wife is sick herself, and Miss Bonner isn't home. Dr. Jordan told me to find a neighbor to stay with us until he gets back here. I came by the post office and picked up the mail, and Charlie was there. So I asked him to come home with me."

"Well, he's just going to add another problem to what's already here," I said.

"He wants to help. Let's give him a chance."

"Where's McKinley?" I asked.

"Went over to see Aunt Leah a minute."

I offered Charlie a chair when he came in the door. He and Dewey sat down together and talked for a minute; then as usual, Dewey bounced off to somewhere else.

Charlie sat in his chair rocking away.

"Sister," he said, "do you need any help?"

"I don't know, Charlie. We're just trying to get Nola better."

"We stopped by Miss Bonner's, and she wasn't home," Charlie said.

"Where could she be in this weather?" Dewey said, bouncing back in the room.

"Hope she's not sick too," I told him.

Dewey got Charlie interested in a game of checkers, and I fell asleep again beside Nola. She seemed to be all right until late afternoon. Then she got fever and chills again. I wished for Daddy and for Dr. Jordan. I tried to feed Nola some broth again, but she refused it.

Dewey put on his milking boots but didn't go to the cow lot. Instead, he announced he was going to walk over to check on Miss Bonner.

"I'll take care of the girls while you're gone," Charlie said.

Charlie Wright could think anything he wanted. I knew who was doing the caretaking.

Dewey was gone about an hour when Charlie got upset about Nola. She was seeing imaginary images. Charlie began pacing and coughing. When he rolled a cigarette, I'd start coughing real loud. I didn't know how to tell someone not to smoke in a sick house. I couldn't get his attention. Finally, I approached him.

"Charlie, Nola is really sick. I think she's getting worse," I said, thinking he would take his cigarette outside.

"You get Nola dressed, Sister," Charlie said and threw his cigarette in the fireplace. "I'm taking her to Dr. Jordan's house."

I struggled with Nola. She felt like a rag doll, limp and heavy, her arms dangling in the air. Finally, I got her fixed to where we could bundle her up. Then I got blankets while Charlie brought the wagon around.

He was fast when he was nervous. He carried Nola to the wagon and covered her up except for her eyes and nose. Charlie seemed frantic, and I started getting my coat on.

"Where is McKinley? Why isn't he over here helping out?" I yelled.

"Sister, McKinley's feeling sick too. What you need to do is stay here and wait for Dewey. If I see him coming, I'll tell him to hurry home."

"Charlie Wright, take care of my little sister."

"Yes, Sister. I'll get her over to Dr. Jordan's real fast."

With that I let him drive off with Nola, knowing Dewey would kill me for letting Charlie take Nola. If he didn't kill me, Daddy would be furious when he got home.

All I had left was the Bible. I got the King James Bible down and opened it up to Psalms 129, verse 12:

Yea, the darkness hideth not from thee,
But the night shineth as the day: the darkness and the light are
Both alike to thee.

Then I sang every song I knew out loud and waited.

CHAPTER 18

HELP FOR NOLA

Someone knocked on the door after dark. It was scary, as the lamp had gone out and the fire had turned to ashes. I had fallen asleep and didn't know where I was.

"You're in your house, Ella. You're waiting for Charlie and Dewey to come back with good news about Nola and Miss Bonner," I told myself, but the knocking got louder.

"Ella!" I heard Aunt Leah's voice shout.

I opened the door and saw my aunt and broke into tears.

"Don't cry, baby. Everything's going to be all right. I just want to take you home with me. Charlie told us he was taking Nola to the doctor's house. I had no idea you would be by yourself so long. Dewey and McKinley are both at our house right now."

Groggily, I stumbled across the road with her. She took me into Kit's room, and it didn't smell like sickness.

"We finally got her over that old flu," Aunt Leah said. "Here's one of Kit's gowns. I want you to get some real sleep tonight."

I was long past caring. What had kept me going had been taken away. I gladly got into the bed on fresh sheets. I didn't ask about Dewey, and I didn't ask about anyone. My eyes closed, and I dreamed about baby Daniel. He was crying loudly as though he was hurting. When I jumped up to check on him, I saw Aunt Leah taking care of Becca who was no longer a baby.

I followed her and sat down at the table. Silently, she started the fire in the stove with one hand while Becca leaned against her. I wanted to help her, but I felt wilted like a thirsty flower.

"Where is everybody?" I asked.

Aunt Leah smiled and brushed hair back off my face with her hand.

"We're waiting until light so Uncle Josh can go see about Nola and Charles. Try not to worry now." She looked at me and started to say something.

"What about Miss Bonner? And when is Daddy coming?" I asked.

"Ella, you were born trying to make the pieces fit in life. Sometimes, they just don't. We don't know where Allibeth is, and we haven't heard from your daddy. It won't be long before we know something, I'm sure."

"But I'm scared Charlie will run off with Nola, and she'll be afraid."

"Charlie has more sense than you give him credit for. He's got a good heart, Ella."

"I'll make the coffee now," I said and filled the pot with water. Coffee milk would be comforting.

When I got the coffee pot bubbling on the stove, Dewey came in. He'd slept in his clothes.

"I'm going back to Miss Bonner's when it gets light," he said. "Maybe she's sick or hurt and needs some help."

"Charlie's gone with the team," I said and motioned for him to pull out some cups. "Daddy will have a conniption fit if you drive the car."

"This is an emergency," he said, and Aunt Leah nodded her head in agreement.

"Then, I'm coming too," I said.

"Too cold," he said. "Only McKinley and I can drive the car. McKinley's under the weather, so as the man of the house, I'll go it alone."

"You better wash your face. You look a mess."

"Don't act like you're my mother," he said.

"Children," Aunt Leah said softly, "don't fight. Remember what your daddy says. Someday you might be oceans apart, and you'll wish you hadn't gotten into scrapes like this."

"Dewey," I said very motherly, "you better take a few sticks of wood to Miss Bonner's."

"I was going to, Sister. Quit bossing me."

"Dew, just run along. Ella and I will have some breakfast fixed when you get back," Aunt Leah said as she washed Becca's face.

"Aunt Leah, can Becca sit by me on the couch?" I asked.

I sat down and looked into her face. She was full of her mother's biscuits, all happy, and cute as a little speckled pup.

"I wonder when we'll get to see Daniel again."

Aunt Leah was busy cooking breakfast and ignored my comment.

"When will we see Daniel again?" I said louder.

"You need to ask your daddy that," she said. Her look told me to stop asking questions.

Kit tottered in as though she was hanging from a fragile thread.

"Are you feeling better?" I asked.

"Yes. Just tired," she said, looking gaunt and colorless.

"I'm glad. Now if everybody else will come home, we'll be all right," I said.

I got my wish. Suddenly somebody banged on the door, and I ran to open it. There stood Charlie!

"Let me get by the fire!" he said.

"Come on in, Charles," Aunt Leah said, motioning him to the fireplace. "Warm your hands."

"Where's Nola?" I asked him.

"Dr. Jordan kept her at his house. He has to give her medicine until she gets well," said Charlie.

Charlie looked like he had been splashed in a mud puddle. I asked him how he had gotten so filthy.

"Well now," Charlie said giggling, "I took Nola over to the doctor's, and he gave me a bed for the night. When I got up this morning, I stepped in a mud hole going out past the door. Then Dr. Jordan told me to come here and tell you he's got Nola with him and Mrs. Jordan."

"But you didn't say how Nola's doing." I said.

"She's sick," Charlie said, "real sick." I had a sinking feeling.

The door opened suddenly, and in barged Dewey, wet from head to foot again.

"Did you find Allibeth?" Aunt Leah asked.

"Yes ma'am, I stopped at her neighbor's, and she was there. Miss Bonner was without firewood at her house."

"But she's okay?"

"She looked all right to me," Dewey said and began to struggle out of his coat.

"Was she sick?" I asked.

"No," he said. "Just cold. So, we went to her house, and I took wood in and built a fire."

"I'll bet she appreciated that," Aunt Leah said.

He laughed. "Yeah, she said I'm getting A's the rest of the year."

While this was going on, I noticed Charlie slumped over on the sofa. I walked over to him.

"Charlie, thank you for taking care of Nola," I said.

"Sure, Sister," Charlie said and leaned his head back to rest a minute. He was off in a dream somewhere, looking up at the ceiling, talking.

"Sis, we better get back home," Dewey said.

I stood up and and plumped the pillows under Becca's head. She was totally asleep.

"Bring your laundry over here," Aunt Leah said. "I'll wash it when the sun comes out for good."

I hoped the sun came out for good today because all our clothes and linens were wet. I hoped the sun came out today so Nola would get better. I hoped the sun came out today because maybe we could hear from Daddy. My heart began pounding in my ears.

CHAPTER 19

FACING THE ENEMY

Nola began to take a favorable turn. She spent a few days and nights at Dr. Jordan's house, and then he sent word that her fever had broken. Later he sent word she was getting some strength again. But he didn't offer to send her back to us. "Us" meant the boys and me, because Daddy had not come home, and no one could locate him.

We tried to make the best of things. We used a sunny day to clean out the sickness in the house. Still, it was full of bad memories.

We ate cornmeal mush every meal and hoped Daddy would get in touch before we ran out of meal. If it hadn't been for Pokey and her milk, we wouldn't have eaten one healthy thing. Heaven forbid that we ask Aunt Leah for more help. If she discovered our sin of gluttony, that would be the end of us.

Miss Bonner came by to go over our lessons with us. She looked around at the disarray, especially in the kitchen, and asked if we needed any help. We said no.

Out of sheer boredom, McKinley started teaching Dewey the guitar. They tried to teach both Miss Bonner and me. I was only interested in singing and couldn't get into it, and Miss Bonner said she was only meant for the piano

Charlie Wright didn't come around much anymore. Someone said he'd had another case of nerves. I asked McKinley if he would drive us to Charlie's house to thank him for saving Nola.

"Ella, I will, but you never know what to expect with Charlie," he said. "Right now, all I'm thinking about is Daddy coming home so we can get some food."

Daddy finally made it. As it turned out, he never got the telegram when Nola was so sick.

He drove Her Majesty over to Dr. Jordan's house to pick up Nola. On the way back to our house, he stopped at Miss Bonner's to thank her for caring for Dewey and me. Daddy was gone a long time.

Dewey and I waited on the porch watching for the car. When it drove up, Nola was sitting beside Daddy. We ran out to them, and Daddy picked Nola up like a baby. He took her in the house with us tagging behind them. I wanted to cheer her up.

"What are white and black and red all over?" I asked her.

"Newspapers," she said weakly and tried to smile. Her eyes were real sunk back, and she was skin and bone.

Daddy put her on the bed and came back in the parlor.

"Let's let her rest a while, children," he said. "This is the first time she's even been outside since she went to Dr. Jordan's."

"Will she be all right?" I asked, looking into her lifeless eyes.

"Yes," he said, "but it was a close call."

"Were you surprised when you found out all that had happened around here, Daddy?" Dewey asked.

"It's just about wrecked me," Daddy said. "If I'd had any idea you children were in such a shape..." His voice broke.

"We made it just fine," Dewey said. "Just fine."

Daddy motioned for us to follow him into the kitchen.

"Guess it's time I go get some groceries," he said, opening and closing the cupboard doors. There's not even a spoonful of flour in this house."

"Or coffee either," I said.

So he and Dewey got in the car and went to town. I checked on Nola, and she was sound asleep. I told myself I would fatten her up as soon as I got the makings for bread.

That night we were all together again. After supper Daddy and the boys got out the instruments and played. They even dedicated some happy songs to Nola and me. Nola had lost all her pluck, and I wanted sleep in the worst way, so everybody said "nighty night" and "don't let the bed bugs bite" and got ready for bed.

We slipped in between the sheets and talked, but we didn't start giggling like we used to do. I tried to cuddle Nola, but she said she was sore all over. That old flu just about ruined my sister. Tomorrow I would start getting some biscuits and gravy down her. She would get nice and plump and healthy again.

After a few days Daddy was called back to work. Nola was getting back to her own healthy self and Daddy was confident we could take care of her. He supplied us with plenty of food and told us to study hard. I told Nola she should start her last reader all over again. She had missed too much learning while she was sick.

When we finally did make it back to school, there was a big crisis: an outbreak of lice. Where those lice came from no one will ever know for sure, but I remember we all went out of our minds scratching our heads. I was afraid I'd done something wrong, so I didn't tell Aunt Leah that I'd scratched my head and made sores all over it.

When she did find out, she came to the rescue.

"Who was the dirty culprit who started this mess? Every child in school is suffering with lice!" she said in a very mean voice.

Lice were parasites that lived in hair. Aunt Leah sat for hours going through our hair picking out nits, washing our hair, and boiling our combs and brushes. The only sure way to get rid of them was to shave the head.

Aunt Leah was not about to shave the girls' heads, although she cut our hair very short. The boys got theirs shaved, and McKinley wore a cap all the time, especially around girls. Dewey blatantly showed his peeled head off and experimented with a remedy for lice. Aunt Leah refused to use it.

Nola and I were both self-conscious about our short hair, but Aunt Leah told us that we both looked cute like that. I knew better, but we were just two of many girls in school who had their tresses cut. I noticed mean Molly Kay had her hair cropped off and by George, she didn't look cute like Aunt Leah said we did. Not that I noticed.

My aunt faithfully doctored our scalps and kept our hair clean. It wasn't easy to wash our hair every day after school and have us sit by the fire until it dried. Sheets, bedclothes, combs, and brushes were boiled as often as possible. But even with Aunt Leah's tender care, my scalp was messed up, and the hair roots weren't coming back in some places. The whole experience was horrifying to me as well as several other girls who didn't know if the hair would truly grow back in. We were at that age where our looks mattered greatly to us whether we cared to admit it or not.

Finally after days of agony and missing school, we got rid of the enemy. It was rumored that a new boy at school who had come down from the mountains had spread these creatures around school. I wasn't sure because I didn't know of a new boy in any of our classes.

Summer came again, and we had a lazy time of it. Daddy wasn't home as often, and we roamed. Dewey was at the age where his voice began to sound two different ways. He never knew when he opened his mouth if he would sound high pitched or low and gravelly. He suddenly acted as if he didn't know Nola and me anymore. The only time he was still was when he was doing his experiments. He stayed at Dr. Jordan's house a lot while Nola, Kit, and I entertained each other.

McKinley was a delivery boy for Hicks Icehouse all summer. We didn't see him except in the evenings. Daddy let him take his girl to the movie house in Her Majesty sometimes.

When Dewey decided he needed a bicycle, Daddy startled us all by suggesting Dew spend the summer with him on the railroad.

"Only thing is, Daddy, what if I ruin my hands shoveling that coal?" Dewey said. "I'm not sure Dr. Jordan would approve. He's big on saving his hands and not doing manual labor. He says a doctor's hands are his life's work, and they should be cared for."

"But I guess it's all right with you and Dr. Jordan if I use my own hands to do hard work day in and day out, right? Dew, pack your bag and let's get going," Daddy said. Daddy laughed out loud when he saw the look of shock on Dew's face.

"Sorry, Daddy," Dew said. "I wasn't thinking straight."

And so one day in late June, Daddy and Dew walked down the road to the station. When they returned in a few weeks, Dewey had a shiny new bike in his possession, and his physician's hands were still unscathed after all the hard labor.

That bicycle would have been the death of anyone other than Dewey. He rode it as if he was going to a fire and stood it up on its back wheel like a stallion raring up. He popped wheelies and made fast turns and became proficient at scaring us all to death.

One day he rode over to Dr. Jordan's to show him one of his experiments and went on out to the country to see how Charlie was doing.

Since none of us knew he was taking a side trip to Charlie's, Daddy began to worry when Dew wasn't back by dark. As it got later and later, he worried some more. Then he decided Dew had probably spent the night with Dr. Jordan because it got too late to ride home on the bicycle.

After we had all fallen asleep, I heard the door creak, and Dewey came in our room.

"Dew, we've been worried about you. Where have you been?" I asked.

"Shhh, Sister, just wait until the morning," he whispered. "Have I got surprise for everyone!"

"Did you bring it on the bike? I didn't hear you ride up on the bike," I said.

"Just wait. You'll never believe it in a million years. Daddy is going to be so proud of me," he said in a croaky whisper.

"Dewey, you smell like a barnyard," I said. "What have you been up to?"

"You'll see in the morning," he said and carefully tiptoed out of the room.

I counted 150 sheep jumping over a fence and still couldn't go to sleep. Finally, just as I was drifting off, I heard Daddy go to the kitchen to make coffee.

CHAPTER 20

THE TRADE-OFF

Nola had to wake me up in the morning. She pulled on my arm and shook me, but I couldn't budge.

"Sister, look out in the front yard!" she yelled excitedly.

I peeked out, and there was a palomino horse tied to our porch. That woke me up fast!

"Oh, my goodness!" I said. "It must be lost."

I hurriedly pulled a dress over my head, and Nola and I nearly tripped over each other getting out the front door. Daddy and McKinley stood on the porch drinking coffee, and they were both quiet—too quiet.

"Daddy, where did you get that horse?" Nola asked.

"You mean, where did Dewey get that horse, don't you? Go in and wake him up, Nola," he said.

Nola made a beeline in to find Dewey, and soon he appeared at the door all smiles.

"Whatta you think?" he asked. "Isn't she a prize?"

"Son," Daddy said, turning slowly around to him, "where in the world did you get a horse?"

Dewey was proud of his accomplishment and began bouncing around.

"Daddy, there's more to this. Let me run out to the barn."

I had never seen Daddy or McKinley without words, but this day was different. We all stood expectantly while Dewey brought his other surprise around.

Soon, here he came leading a colt. Dewey had his biggest smile on.

"Look at this little lady. That's what I'm gonna call her: Lady," he said, full of himself.

"Hold on, Dew. First, how did you get these two horses?" Daddy said, as Nola and I stood ooohing and ahhhhing.

"Bartered for them," Dewey said.

"I can't imagine what you traded, Dewey. You don't have anything to trade," Daddy said.

"Traded my bike to Charlie," he said. "Charlie gave me his daddy's horse and new colt for it. Said his pa wouldn't mind."

"Oh, good Lord, Dewey, you get those horses and take them right back to Charles Wright. First, they aren't his to trade; they're his folks' animals. Second, we don't have a place to keep horses, and third, I thought you wanted that bicycle more than anything!"

Daddy had a shouting voice going now, and Dewey looked confused.

"I feel like giving you a thrashing, Dewey. Instead, I'm going to take a drive out to the Wrights and apologize, and you're going to lead those horses all the way out there and ride your bicycle back here."

"I'll go with you now, Daddy," Dewey said. "No sense in getting Charlie in trouble. He thought he was doing right."

Daddy stiffened his back, stepped inside the door, and yelled, "Dewey, I need to be by myself awhile. I'm mad right now."

"But Daddy, it wasn't my fault. After I stopped at Dr. Jordan's, I decided to cheer Charlie up and let him ride my bike. So, I went all the way out to their farm, and Charlie wanted the bike. He said he'd trade me the horses for it. Mr. and Mrs. Wright were out in their cotton patch, so we couldn't ask them because they were busy."

Dew kept on explaining to the air, because Daddy was already cranking Her Majesty. Dewey was upset.

When Daddy drove off, we all felt sorry for Dewey. He thought he had done something fine.

"Can we at least pet them?" Nola said. "They look gentle."

"Go ahead," Dewey said, sniffing. "That mare is pretty old and slow, but I'd be careful with the colt."

"That mare was not too old to have a colt!" Nola said.

McKinley put his arm around Dewey, because blood is thicker than water. Those two could fight each other, but they held each other up when push came to shove.

I knew horses liked sugar cubes, but we couldn't find anything at all for a treat. Nola and I spent the morning patting them and talking to them as if they were babies. The boys led them back and forth a lot so the mare could nibble grass. I even asked if I could braid the mare's tail, but Dewey said no.

Daddy was gone a long time. When he came back, he put away Her Majesty and asked Dewey to get the wagon and team ready.

"This is going to be a slow trip," he said. "We'll tie the mare and colt to the sides of the wagon, and you boys can ride in the back and watch out for them. I'll drive the team, and when we get to the Wrights,' we'll pick up the bicycle and bring it home."

"Why do I have to go?" McKinley said. "I'm supposed to be going to the picture show tonight with the gang."

"Because I said so," Daddy said in exasperation. "Now, that's the end of it."

They had trouble getting the mare and her colt to separate because the colt wanted to nurse. Finally, the boys tied them to each side of the wagon and found their places inside it. Dewey looked shattered, McKinley looked sullen, and Daddy stared straight ahead.

Nola and I watched as the wagon went slowly down the road along with Dewey's first failed business transaction.

"I sure wanted my picture made on that horse," Nola said sadly, watching them leave. "Everybody but us gets to have their picture made on a horse."

CHAPTER 21

AT ODDS WITH CIRCUMSTANCES

That summer Nola and I walked to town every day. Daddy set us up a charge account at the Dalby Brothers Grocery and told us we could put groceries on his monthly bill. At the end of the month, he paid the store for what we'd bought. The first bill came in with mostly candy and goodies charged to Daddy. McKinley got in big trouble for allowing it when Daddy came home, so we got more sensible after that.

The hot days wore lazily on. We were wet with perspiration half the time. When there was no wind blowing, we burned up.

Daddy came home from the railroad one day, and Charlie was walking with him. He had his gun, so I guessed he was looking for squirrels again.

"No, Sister," he said when I asked him, "I'm looking for them cotton pickers that beat me up."

"It's not quite time for them, Charlie," Daddy said. "Give 'em another month. Now, you go set that gun down and come in for some coffee."

That's when we learned that the law was going to put Charlie in an asylum.

"What's an asylum?" Nola asked.

"Don't know what it's like, but the law says I have to go for a while. Says I'm too mad at the world, and I'm going to hurt somebody one of these days."

Daddy touched him on the shoulder. "Now, Son, I think that's a little drastic. I know your mama and daddy wouldn't allow the law to send you away."

Charlie rolled a cigarette, and Daddy lit his pipe. Charlie's hand was shaking, and he began talking out loud to himself.

"Come on, Son, let me take you home. Girls, come with me," Daddy said.

So Daddy drove us all in Her Majesty to make Charlie feel lighter inside. When we got to his house, his parents were sitting on the porch. Nola wanted to stay in the car out of mere contrariness, but in my role as the Rock, I walked up the porch steps with Daddy and Dew.

"How are you?" said Mrs. Wright, rocking back and forth in her chair. She looked too old to be a mother, more like a grandmother. Her gray hair was knotted into a tight bun at the back of her head. Her face was weathered from the sun and lined with frown-caused wrinkles.

"Mighty fine, ma'am," Daddy said. "Just thought I'd bring your boy home."

Charlie was getting out of the car as fast as he could. It was as though his parents were invisible because he didn't acknowledge them.

"Everything all right?" asked Mr. Wright in a voice expecting trouble.

"No, he's just nervous, that's all," Daddy said.

"How's Nola?" asked Mrs. Wright.

"She's doing pretty well; in fact, that's her waiting for us in the car. You know how children are—one way one minute and another the next."

"Charles is fond of yore children, Jim," Mrs. Wright said.

"They're fond of Charlie too, Mrs. Wright. He probably saved Nola's life, if the truth were known. On another note, to his credit, he's quite a musician, and the boys like playing with him."

"Such a shame, such a shame," Mrs. Wright said. "Learned to play every instrument we have by ear on his own. Then the accident had to happen to him. Don't guess he'll ever be right."

"Don't give up hope," I chimed in. "And I hope he doesn't have to go to that asylum."

Daddy was standing beside me and dug his fingers gently into my shoulder. I got "the look" to be quiet.

When we went back to the car to leave, I pouted. Daddy shouldn't have gotten on to me. Charlie saved Nola's life, and he was good to us in his own way.

"Daddy, why did you pinch me?" I asked.

"You weren't minding your own business," he said, frowning and looking straight ahead.

"Somebody had to speak up for Charlie," I said.

"It's not our business, Sister. Now, hold your tongue!"

We rode along in silence, and I continued to pout. When we passed by Miss Bonner's house, Nola asked if we could go in and see her.

"Why not?" Daddy said and smiled.

He stopped and began getting out of the car with Nola. I stayed put, still angry with Daddy.

"Ella, get out of the car. You need to start minding your manners and respecting your elders," Daddy said.

"Mind your own," I said low under my breath.

Daddy whipped around. "What did you say, young lady?"

I was a bad liar, so I admitted my slipup. Daddy told me he was tired of my back talk. I sat still knowing I would get punished.

Nola yelled at me to come on, and Daddy was looking at me red faced.

About that time Miss Bonner walked out the door. Her face showed approval for us stopping, because she always turned pink when Daddy came around.

"Just in time, Jim," she said. "I made a peach cobbler. Y'all come on in."

Whew, I'd been saved from my doom. Maybe Daddy would forget my talking back to him.

The dessert and visit went splendidly until Daddy said he had to take us home. He told Miss Bonner he had a little discipline problem to see to.

Miss Bonner looked sad, but she told us good-bye, and we were off to the house. When we got there, Daddy told me to go pull a switch off a tree and bring it to him.

I was afraid. Since Daddy had only given me two spankings in my life, I was expecting some leniency. My bottom was certain to be black and blue!

"I didn't aim to talk back to you, Daddy," I cried.

"Now, Ella, I don't believe in whipping girls. But, you just went too far with me. You need to remember this lesson."

"The damage is done. Now, you go get that switch," he said.

Nola went in the house so happy to blab to Dewey I was getting whipped. I would give her one cold shoulder now.

I picked the smallest switch I could and took it in to Daddy. He told me to turn around and whacked me twice across my legs.

"This hurts me more than it hurts you, Sister. I'm doing this for your own good. You know the Bible says the tongue is our worst enemy. I hope you understand what you said was bad. You don't talk back to your elders."

I told him yes sir and ran to the bedroom. I didn't cry because I wanted to show Daddy I was tough. But the little switch only made the whipping hurt more. Oh, Daddy would be sorry for this. I wouldn't speak to him the rest of the day or maybe forever!

When I heard noise outside, I perked up my ears. It was Kit and Nola playing jump rope, and I was jealous they were having so much fun. I walked out on the porch with my saddest face on.

"Wanta play, Ella?" asked Kit.

"She just wants to pout," Nola said with satisfaction.

"Do not!" I said and tried not to cry.

"Did your whipping hurt?" taunted my little sister.

"What do you think?" I said.

"That'll teach you to talk back to your elders," she said. With that, I shoved her down, and she screamed at the top of her lungs.

Daddy bounded through the door angrily.

"Ella, what is going on out there? Don't be hitting on Nola."

"But it's not just me making trouble," I told him.

"Don't you think I know that? I just don't want you to get in the habit of acting ugly," he said.

With that, he sat me down and explained it was his job to teach me to be a good person.

"To tell you the truth, I don't care how you treat me, because I know you don't mean it. But if you practice these bad habits, you won't know how to treat other people. Now, I want you to go off to your room and think about what I've said. When you've thought it over, and understand it, you can come and join the family."

It didn't take long in that room to come to an understanding with myself, because I was getting bored. So, I came out, slunk by Daddy, and went out to play.

The next few days were heaven on earth with the good mood in the house, clean clothes, and plenty of food.

We got an extra happy surprise when Daddy told us he would be around some extra days this trip.

"So you can help us get ready for our new school year?" Nola asked.

"In a way," he said. "I just have some matters to take care of before I go back to work."

I secretly wished he would start courting Miss Bonner. But I wasn't about to open my mouth and stick my big foot in it. Luckily, Dewey came through in a big way.

"Daddy, do you ever think you'll marry again?"

Daddy looked at him strangely. "Maybe," he said.

"How about if you marry Miss Bonner?" Dewey said.

"Miss Bonner isn't allowed to marry," Daddy said.

"Why not?" Dewey asked.

"She's a teacher," Daddy said. "Women teachers can't marry. If they do, they have to give up their jobs. Miss Bonner doesn't want to give up her job."

"How do you know that, Daddy?" I asked.

"Ella, are you being sarcastic to me again?" he asked and sighed noisily.

"I don't think so," I stuttered. "What does sarcastic mean?"

"It means disrespecting your elders, in this case."

"I didn't mean to, Daddy," I said.

"Okay, hon," he said."I have things on my mind right now. Serious things. You may get to help me sort them out."

We were all very quiet. Something had hit a nerve with Daddy. There was something about Miss Bonner he wasn't telling us.

We had a long several days with Daddy, but he was quiet and somber. Grown-ups, I decided, held things inside themselves. There was an air of sadness around the house with him like that. He didn't even play his music.

Nola and I took walks with Kit every day. When I told Kit about Charlie going to an asylum, her eyes got really big.

"Let's go to his house and see if he's still around," she said.

"I hope his parents changed their minds," I said remembering how I'd gone out on a limb to make that suggestion to them. I had bruises on my legs to prove it.

We decided to ask Charlie to go fishing, so we gathered up our fishing poles, and Dewey got the wagon ready to go to the Wrights.

"I'll wait for y'all in the wagon," Dewey said. "Just get a move on."

When we got to the house, Nola knocked on the door while Kit and I stood behind her.

"Mrs. Wright?" she said.

"Hello, Nola," Mrs. Wright said in a flat tone. Her eyes had no feeling showing.

"Can Charlie go fishing with us?" Nola asked.

"Sorry, Nola," Mrs. Wright said dully, "the law is coming in a little while to take him over to the asylum in Little Rock."

"Can we see him?" Nola asked.

"It would make him too nervous," Mrs. Wright said.

"It won't make him nervous to see us," Nola said. "He likes us."

Mrs. Wright opened the door and motioned us into her front room.

"Charles! Charles!" she called. "Come on out. You have company."

But there wasn't time, because the sheriff drove up and knocked on the door. Mrs. Wright took the sheriff back to Charlie's room. He told her he needed to talk to Charlie alone, and she walked down the hall toward us.

Suddenly we heard a gunshot and glass shattering.

CHAPTER 22
WHEN BAD THINGS HAPPEN

N ola and Kit jumped up and started to run out the door
screaming, but I sat glued to my chair.

"Mrs. Wright!" the sheriff yelled. "Come in here!"

She ran down the hall, and I heard her cry out. I stood up shak-
ily to run out to the lawn with the girls, but a commotion started in
the hallway. I looked around frantically.

Charles walked out with the sheriff on one side of him and his
mother on the other. They led him down the hall toward me. I was
so shocked to see the three of them walking on their own two feet
together that I started crying.

I looked up at Charlie through my tears, but he looked right
through me. His hands were trembling as he fumbled for his tobacco in his pocket. It was the saddest sight I'd ever seen.

"Don't take him away!" I cried. "I've heard about that old asylum, and Charlie doesn't belong there!"

"He'll be just fine, little lady," the sheriff said very businesslike,
and he opened the door for Charlie to go out.

I went outside with the girls, all of us crying. The sheriff seemed
to be nice enough to Charlie. He put him beside him in the car
and asked if he was comfortable.

Kit, Nola, and I held on to each other, still crying. Dewey was in the yard now too and stood staring into the distance like he was somewhere else. I watched Charlie through water. He had given up.

I wondered what he was thinking.

Mrs. Wright stood at the door wiping her eyes.

"What happened?" Kit asked her.

"He shot a hole through the mirror. When the sheriff walked into his room, he thought it was those boys that beat him in the reflection."

"Nobody was hurt?" Nola asked.

"Every one of us is hurting. I ask myself every day why my boy had to be the one to have something wrong with his brain."

"We'll stay with you until Mr. Wright gets back," I offered.

"No, thank you," she said. "I need some time alone with my thoughts."

She gave us each a handkerchief, and we dried our tears. Then we picked up our fishing poles from the ground that never got used and got in the wagon to go home. Somehow, it didn't seem fair that we should get to go fishing when Charlie had to go to the asylum.

Mrs. Wright sat down in her rocker as Dew steered the team to the road. She stared off into the distance like she was thinking really hard.

When we got home, Daddy came out to meet us.

"Why does God do bad things to people?" Nola asked.

"God never does bad things to people," Daddy said.

"But Charlie…" Nola said.

"Bad things happen because somewhere down the line, people made wrong choices," Daddy said.

"I don't understand," I said.

"You can ask God about it someday," he said gently.

CHAPTER 23

SUNDAY AFTERNOONS

Sometimes a girl needed a mama, and lonely Sunday afternoons were some of those times. After Daddy left for the railroad and the boys got involved in their own lives, Nola and I often searched for something to do.

"Nola, let's grab Kit and walk to the cemetery and say hey to Mama," I said one Sunday afternoon.

"Sister, do you think that'll make us feel any better? She can't talk to us. She's not even in that grave anymore," Nola said wistfully.

"Still, we can talk to her," I said.

"Okay," she said, "but don't get to scaring me in the graveyard."

"I won't," I said, because I got a little antsy in cemeteries myself.

Kit was more than glad to go with us. She said she was bored and was tired of helping out with Becca.

The roses were blooming on the fence, and someone had dug a fresh grave nearby. We walked to where Mama lay and looked at her new tombstone. The etched inscription read, "Beloved Rebeccah, nuna-da-ul-tsun-yi" to honor her heritage as a Cherokee descendent.

"We miss you, Mama," Nola said and looked stricken.

I didn't know Nola would take this so hard. I was usually so busy being the rock and woman of the house, I tried not to think of Mama too much. But a certain part of life was empty without her and some nights I dreamed she was with us.

I hugged Nola and pointed to the road.

"Look who's coming with a big bouquet of flowers," I said. "Troy Clark!"

"Are you all right?" he asked Nola.

"No," she said.

"You look awful sad," he said.

"We're thinking about our mama," I told him.

"I know. My mama's right over there," he said pointing to a grave not far away.

"We've got to get home," I said. The graveyard was making me feel weird.

"Well, why don't you say 'so long' to your mama, and I'll walk you back home. I want to go see McKinley anyway," he said.

"Did you bring those flowers for your mama?" I asked.

"Yes, but I just got this feeling she wants me to share them with you."

He handed each of us a pungent red summer rose and started walking to his mother's grave.

"Don't step on a grave!" Kit yelled. "It's bad luck!"

"Bad manners too," he said and laughed.

Troy zigzagged us between the graves so we wouldn't have bad luck. He knelt down beside his mother's, crossed himself, and mouthed silent words. Then he stood up and started walking us out to the road.

When we got outside the cemetery, we all started talking at once, and we even got to laughing.

"Are you playing baseball this summer?" I asked, knowing Troy was an expert at playing any ball sport, be it foot, base, or basket.

"I missed out on it this summer," he said. "I have to work at Hicks to save some money. One of these days, Mack and I are going to start a band, and that won't even seem like working."

"Can I be your singer?" I asked.

"Sure," he said and winked at me with eyes the color of Miss Bonner's opal ring.

McKinley wasn't as happy to see us as he was to see Troy. They went out in the yard and started throwing a ball back and forth to each other and talking about their summer at the icehouse.

"Were you born here in Pine Bluff?" McKinley asked.

"Yep, and so were my two sisters. They're a lot older than me and already married," he said.

"How's it working out with just you and your dad?" McKinley asked.

"Dad's best friend is the bottle," Troy answered. "He's about half alive from all the moonshine he drinks. Never touched it until Mom died."

They stopped throwing the ball and walked over to the porch steps. Troy sat there for a minute looking down at his feet.

"Hey, Dew! Get your fiddle, and let's make some music!" McKinley yelled.

In five minutes flat, they were tuning up and making music.

Music, I thought, is better than any medicine to make a person feel better.

Kit and I harmonized, and Nola looked through a book. Suddenly, Kit stopped, looked at the road, and closed her eyes tightly.

"See a bale of hay, make a wish and look away!" she said.

I saw a wagon pass with bales of hay piled on it.

"Hurry, Ella, make a wish!" she yelled.

I squeezed my eyes shut and wished that someday I'd marry Troy Clark.

"Open them now!" she said. "It'll come true if you don't see the hay again."

When I opened my eyes, I glanced over in the direction of the wagon and saw the hay. I wasn't going to get my wish to marry Troy.

"I don't believe that stuff anyway," I said.

"Oh, I do," said Kit. "You'll never believe in a million years what I wished for."

Aunt Leah interrupted our conversation when she walked across the road with Becca. "Come on home, Kit. Ella, you and Nola get your gowns and come spend the night at my house."

Nola and I surely hated to leave the house with Troy Clark in it. I was in love for the first time, and I just knew Troy would be my husband some day. He could play in McKinley's band, and I could be the singer. The only problem was, how were Kit and I both going to marry him? It was apparent from her expression that she was as smitten with him as I was.

The next morning Troy Clark walked down the road to go back home. But he and McKinley had made plans during the night to start a band. I told Kit Troy said I could be a singer for them and maybe she could too.

"Mm-hm," she said. "I'm going to be his wife and his singer," she said.

We didn't mind sharing true love. We were best friends.

CHAPTER 24

NEW SCHOOL YEAR

We started school in September. I was excited about being older and learning something new. Lots of children complained about school, especially my sister, but she wasn't the one keeping things going at home like me, the Rock. I was anxious to start collecting books like the boys did, so my goal was to read well to impress Daddy. Daddy encouraged the boys to select Mark Twain books, I guess, because Samuel Clements had worked on a riverboat as he had.

Miss Bonner didn't seem as friendly anymore. Last year she had gone out of her way to welcome my siblings and me. This year we were just students in her class. I didn't worry myself about it, but I did wonder.

Dewey tried to teach me how to play the fiddle. I would place it under my chin, aim the bow, and make a squeak.

"Dad burn it, Ella, I told you how to do E, A, D, and G. Here we go again. Place that finger on that string and that finger on the other one. And keep your fingers off the horsehair on the bow. It'll get oil on it!"

"Didn't know the bow had horsehair on it. Besides, I don't want to learn the fiddle. I want to sing."

"You need to know your notes if you're going to be a singer, Sister," he said.

"I can pick up a melody. Don't need no music to go by," I said playfully.

"Quit talking like a cotton picker," he said.

I surely wanted to know a cotton picker. I thought they must be mean and not able to talk very well either.

Saturdays after baths, we all spent the night at Aunt Leah's. We helped Aunt Leah fix food for Sunday dinner, and sometimes tears came to my eyes as I thought back to Mama's nature, very sweet like Aunt Leah's.

After the lamps were turned off, we three girls piled up in bed together. One of us would start giggling and couldn't stop. Eventually Aunt Leah threatened to wear us out before we settled down. Aunt Leah said she liked having us for company while Uncle Josh was at the sawmill working, but I know we tried her patience.

One Saturday she came in with a letter from Daddy. He would be home the first of October with some important news. He had been talking about buying a place in the country, so I imagined that was his news.

When he got home, the leaves were turning golden and red. The hot summer had disappeared, and in its place were apples on the trees and cider to be made. Aunt Leah had the apple trees, and we picked and ate them straight from the branches.

Daddy was happy to be home and happy to drink some fresh cider. I asked him if he'd like to have a dance.

"No, Sister," he said. "My time isn't long this round. I just need to talk to you children and tell you about some plans I have."

He didn't look worried, so I thought life must be looking up for him. In fact, he looked downright pleased with himself.

That night after supper, he gathered us on the porch and prepared us for the future.

"How would you feel about moving to Little Rock?" he asked.

"No, I don't want to," Nola said quickly.

"I can't. Dr. Jordan needs me," Dewey said, throwing a ball against the side of the house.

"I don't want to go to a different school. Besides, what would Aunt Leah do without us?" was my response.

"So, I guess that's a no?" he said.

"Right," I said. "Let's don't even think about it."

"Not much choice, Sister," he said. "I've met someone I'd like to marry."

"I'll bet Miss Bonner decided to stop teaching school and marry us," I said.

"No, it's not Miss Bonner; it's a nice lady in Little Rock."

"I'm not moving," Nola said.

"Me neither," I said.

"That makes three of us," Dewey said. "I need to stay here and learn doctoring."

"I'll bet McKinley won't move. He has friends he won't want to leave," I said.

"Well, children, we're moving after Christmas. So set your minds to thinking about it. Nobody is staying here."

He got up and started in the house but stuck his head out the door.

"You'll like her," he said. "Her name's Rhodie."

There was no way I could get my head on straight thinking about a new mama coming into our family, and a stranger at that. So I decided to not think about it. Daddy might change his mind anyway, and it was God's will, whatever happened.

"I knew it! I knew it!" Kit said when I told her the news.

"How did you know?" I asked her.

"I counted ten buzzards in the sky a few days ago, and that means a wedding in the spring."

Daddy said Kit was a mighty superstitious girl, and I shouldn't take her sayings seriously. But this one came true. She had been counting buzzards again.

If Kit saw ten buzzards, that definitely meant Daddy would marry that Rhodie woman next spring. We would be living in Little Rock, Arkansas. That was a world away from Pine Bluff.

"What do you think this Miss Rhodie is like?" Dewey asked me.

"I'll bet she's pretty," I said. "Daddy likes pretty."

"She's probably a good cook too," said Dewey. "He loves food."

Still, I thought Daddy surely wouldn't take us away from Aunt Leah and Kit and Miss Bonner and our fishing hole.

We didn't know what to expect the day we went to Little Rock. Daddy had us all dress up and squished us into Her Majesty. He was merry and sang songs as we drove along. I sang right along with him but still I thought we would never get there.

We pulled up to what looked like a mansion to me. Daddy got out of the car and motioned with his hand for us to stay put. When he walked up the porch, a stout woman with dark-brown hair came out. Nola kept her eyes on the porch, but I looked away.

"He's hugging her," Nola whispered, her eyes wide. "That must be Rhodie."

Then Daddy brought her out to the car.

"I'd like you to meet a friend of mine," Daddy said. "This is Miss Rhodie; and Rhodie, this is my brood: McKinley, Dewey, Ella, and Nola. Say hello to Miss Rhodie!"

We stepped out of the car, and the boys took off their hats.

"Nice to meet you, ma'am," said Dewey, who was glad to be out of the car so he could bounce around

McKinley nodded to her and said, "Hello, Miss Rhodie."

But Nola and I were speechless.

Miss Rhodie looked like one of the women who attended our church. Dark-brown hair piled on top of her head, eyes so deep brown the center didn't show, and a solid, sturdy figure. She walked over to Nola and me.

"I've heard a lot about you girls," she said and bent down to hug us. She smelled nice, like rose water. "Come, let's go in the house and meet Lethie."

Daddy had told us about Lethie, who was Miss Rhodie's housekeeper.

"How in tarnation did Daddy find *her?*" whispered Nola as Rhodie went back over and took Daddy's arm.

"Shhhh," I whispered back and looked pointedly at her to lower her voice.

"I don't like her!" Nola said.

"Why? You don't even know her," I said.

"I'm tired of Daddy always having secrets. It's not fair."

"She's not a secret, Nola."

"That's for sure. See the way they're looking at each other, Sister?" she said.

I felt exactly like Nola did, but I tried hard to hide it. For the first time, a strange feeling came over me, and I knew what *jealous* meant.

Lethie was waiting for us inside the house. She had the biggest smile with a space between her front teeth. She wasn't shy at all and hugged each one of us long and hard.

"You chillin hongry?" she asked. "I fried you up some chicken and made you a punkin pie. Come on in the kitchen, honeys, while Rhodie and Jim visit."

"Are you Miss Rhodie's sister?" Nola asked as Lethie held her hand and led her to a chair.

She chuckled. "No ma'am, I work for Miss Rhodie keeping her house and doing the cooking. Been around this house since Rhodie was a baby."

As we ate, Lethie told us about Little Rock.

"Turning into a real big town. We have a fine school here. There's a library in town where you can even borrow books."

Daddy popped his head in the door. "Y'all about finished? We have to get back home before dark."

"Okay, Daddy, but can we stop by that record store?" Dewey asked.

"I'll pick some up next time we're here. Just not enough time today," Daddy said, smiling at Miss Rhodie.

It was obvious McKinley was ready. He got into Her Majesty as soon as Daddy said "go."

Miss Rhodie hugged us all as if she actually knew us and waved as if she cared a lot. I just hoped it was the real thing, but I wasn't buying it yet.

When we drove away, I asked Daddy if we could stop by the asylum and see Charlie Wright.

"We'll visit Charlie one of these days, Sister," he said. "It would be out of our way to stop there today."

"He's probably happy in that asylum," Nola said. "I'll bet he's playing his guitar and making music."

Daddy agreed that he probably was.

CHAPTER 25

A NEW MOTHER IDEA

We had good family time with Daddy being home. I forgot about moving to Little Rock. He even let McKinley take us to school in Her Majesty some days.

Our curiosity was huge about how Daddy and Miss Rhodie had gotten to know each other. We finally got Kit to ask because she wouldn't get in trouble.

"Uncle Jim, I always thought Miss Bonner was kind of like your girlfriend," she said. "I was just wondering how you met Miss Rhodie."

He cleared his throat. "I met her one day in Oklahoma. We liked each other almost instantly," he said. "She'll make a fine mother to the children."

Daddy wasn't about to dispense any information to us.

"Then, what about Miss Bonner? She's nice and would make a good mother."

"We're only friends, Kit," he said. He got up and began raking leaves in the yard.

"Hmm, that's the end of that," said Kit, looking at me.

One Sunday afternoon after church, Miss Bonner happened by. We were all sitting on the porch admiring the dinner we'd just had, complaining about how full we were.

"Afternoon, Jim," Miss Bonner said without smiling as she walked by.

"Afternoon, Alli," Daddy said. "Come join us. I was just about to get the guitar out."

"No, I don't think it would be proper under the circumstances," she said.

"Please, Miss Bonner!" I said. "We've missed you this summer. And we're moving to Little Rock in early winter!"

"So I hear," she said without smiling. She seemed miffed.

"Oh, come on, Alli. Be a sport. These children want your company, and so do I. What brings you out on a walk on a hot afternoon like this one?"

"I thought you were probably gone by now, and I was checking on the children," she said, evading Daddy's eyes.

"We have some fudge I made yesterday afternoon," I said. "It'll make your toenails curl."

She smiled then and came on in through the gate.

"All right." She smiled. "Since you put it that way, Ella."

By the time that afternoon ended, the plate of fudge was long gone, and Daddy had used up all the songs he knew. Miss Bonner even got to laughing and singing with us. Whatever had made her angry was not known, but she was in a good mood by the time she left. Daddy offered to drive her, but she politely refused.

"I wish she could be your wife instead of that Miss Rhodie," Nola said.

My heart nearly jumped out of my chest. She was cruising for a bruising.

"Nola, Miss Bonner and I are just friends. You'll come to love Miss Rhodie. I promise."

We continued on in school, all of us in earshot of each other in class. I was afraid Miss Bonner would take out her frustration with Daddy on us. But she was fair to all of us in every way.

As time went on, I almost forgot about the plan to move to Little Rock. The boys had their own lives, and Nola became enthralled with young Becca. I spent a lot of time getting to know my own self.

One day when I was all alone, Mrs. Harlen came by the house with another load of clothes she had collected from the church. Since Daddy and the boys weren't home, I got my chance to speak my mind.

"Mrs. Harlen," I said, "we don't need clothes. My daddy is managing fine to provide for us."

Nola came through the door from Aunt Leah's just as Mrs. Harlen started speaking.

"Why, Ella, these clothes are practically brand-new. They're from a good family who takes pride in appearance," she said.

"Daddy's going to buy me a red dress and a red hat and some red shoes," Nola said. "We don't need any hand-me-downs."

"Nolaaaaaa," I said, emphasizing the error of her ways.

"I'm leaving them here anyway," Mrs. Harlen said. "Be ungrateful if you wish. And your daddy will hear about how you acted."

"Fine by me," Nola said. "It was your fault Mrs. Terrill took off with our baby."

"What are you talking about?" she said. Her face turned red, and veins stuck out on her neck.

"If it hadn't been for you, Mrs. Terrill would never have thought about taking Daniel away," I told her.

She dropped the bundle of clothes on the settee and huffed out the door. She muttered to herself all the way out the gate. I felt really sorry that we had acted so ugly to her when she was trying to help us. I hoped Daddy wouldn't find out that we acted so rudely.

When she left, Nola spied a red dress in the bundle. She pulled it out and held it up in front of her.

"This is pretty," she conceded.

"Too big for you, Nola. Don't even think about it," I said.

"Then I'll get Aunt Leah to take it up," she said.

"You have no pride, Nola," I told her.

"You wouldn't let me wear that other red dress Mrs. Harlen brought," she screamed. "I've always wanted a red dress!"

And so it went. Aunt Leah made some adjustments on the dress and made it fit Nola. She put that dress on every day for a week. I buried the rest of the bundle in a trash pile Daddy was going to burn. I didn't want her to pick out any other dresses that someone else had before us. It felt too shameful.

On Sunday we planned to go to church with Aunt Leah and Uncle Josh. Nola poked along and wouldn't get ready.

"Nola, if you don't get ready, we're going without you," Dewey said.

"Fine by me. Go ahead," she said.

We walked over to Aunt Leah's, minus Nola, and all headed for church. We went to our special pew, and I kept looking to the back of the church for Nola. We sang our first hymn, and no Nola. Someone said a long prayer, and when I opened my eyes, Nola was beside me. To my anguish, she was in her new hand-me-down dress.

I gave her the look, but she ignored me.

When church ended, Mrs. Harlen came by and told Nola how pretty she looked.

"Don't you think Nola looks wonderful in red?" Mrs. Harlen said to the preacher's wife.

"Just darling," said the church's first lady. The crowd milled around outside visiting. The women were discussing their hats and such, and the men were lighting cigarettes. As much as I was used to Daddy's pipe, it seemed odd that a man couldn't wait until he got out of sight of the church to smoke.

Suddenly, one of the older girls ran up to Nola. "You've got on my dress!" she shrieked.

Nola tried to fade into oblivion, but the red dress stood out like a sore thumb.

"This is what you gave to the church, Jo," Mrs. Harlen told the girl. "By your charity, someone is making use of something that doesn't fit you anymore."

There was that word again: charity. Mrs. Harlen had sworn to Daddy that her actions were not charity.

"Come on, Nola, let's go home," I whispered. I got her arm, and we walked as fast as we could to get away from church.

"I told you not to wear that dumb dress," I said.

"I know," she said quietly and went off to the back of the house. I left her there for a while, and when I went back to check on her, she had taken the scissors to the red dress. She cut it up and threw it in the trash pile.

"Red's not my color anymore," she said quietly.

CHAPTER 26

HELP FROM MISS BONNER

One day at school, I asked Miss Bonner for help on my arithmetic. That request rekindled the old friendship we'd had before Miss Rhodie came into the picture.

She came by the house one day while Daddy was on the railroad.

"I'd like to help you children in your studies," she said.

"Oh, would you? This arithmetic won't stick in my head."

"You're too hard on yourself, Ella. Let's go through the steps we worked on in class today."

It wasn't my idea of fun to work on numbers after school every day, but Miss Bonner was willing to help, so I had to adapt. Finally, I began to understand some of it, but the very next day, we started on another hopeless problem. Miss Bonner stayed with it though; I'll give her credit for that.

One day as I was working, I asked Miss Bonner if she had heard from the Terrills.

"Not in a long time," she said. "The last letter I sent came back saying, 'address unknown.'"

"She stole Daniel," I said.

"Ella, I think the Terrills and your father worked out something together on Daniel. Don't you think the baby is better off with a mother who can take care of him?"

"He's our blood, and it's not right," I said.

"Dear, let's just concentrate on your work and not your worries," she said.

"I can't help but think about Daniel," I said.

"Just try to do the best you can in your arithmetic," she said. "Little Rock has a better school than the one you're in. It'll be a challenge unless you work really hard until you move."

Miss Bonner stopped talking and stared out the window. I couldn't think of anything to say, because I was as unhappy as she was about our moving.

CHAPTER 27

MOVING AWAY

We worked for two days packing up our things to move to Little Rock. Daddy stored most of the furniture in Aunt Leah's shed. She also offered to keep an eye on our place. He gave Pokey away, and Aunt Leah kept Callie.

Dewey happily agreed to drive Her Majesty. Daddy wanted to steer the wagon since it was loaded with all our personal belongings.

Aunt Leah and Kit stood on the porch waving as we drove away, all of us like little clouds in the sky letting off water. Nola rode with Daddy, and I rode with the boys.

Dewey drove at first, and we had fun following the wagon. He was great at remembering jokes, and I was a good laugher. When we got really bored, we sang to our heart's content. McKinley read *Call of the Wild* aloud to us until his mouth got too dry to talk.

It took us two full daylight-to-dark days to get to Miss Rhodie's. Our mules, like Pokey, were getting old, so we had to camp one night. Daddy switched vehicles with us when we got closer to Little Rock. He said Dewey was about to run over the wagon with the car.

Finally, we saw the outskirts of Little Rock, Arkansas, the capitol of our great state, as Charlie would say. It made me all squishy in my stomach wondering about our new stepmother.

We were soiled and cranky and hungry by the time we got there. Daddy pulled to a stop in front of the house, and Dewey stopped the team. Daddy got out of the car and stood on one foot and then the other to get a charley horse out of his leg. We noticed McKinley was still reading his book as though nothing was happening.

Then Daddy bounded up the steps of the porch, and we watched as the door swung open.

"I can't believe it! You're finally here!" said a high-pitched, joyful voice.

Daddy stepped inside, and we waited silently. Finally, out came the beauteous housekeeper with coffee-and-cream-colored skin. She had her widest smile on, and she began motioning for us to come in.

"Why you sit in dat car, younguns? Come here and give Lethie a hug," she said.

Then out walked Daddy arm in arm with Miss Rhodie. He was looking down at her with crinkled, smiling eyes, and she was looking up at him like he was one of those new movie stars.

Meanwhile, Lethie was opening the car door, helping us out and picking up things to carry in.

"Follow me, chillen," she said. "I'll show you where to put your thangs."

Daddy reintroduced us as we came up the steps. We were all polite. I could hardly wait to get a better look at Miss Rhodie.

The boys helped Daddy carry our trunks upstairs to our new room. He had his own room down the hall.

"This is pretty," I said as I looked around our room. The drapes were long and silky and felt soft. "I wonder when they're getting married."

Nola pouted. "I hope never. I don't like this place, and I hope we leave tomorrow."

Through the window, I saw Dewey already outside investigating. I knew he couldn't sit still inside a house.

At supper-time there was enough food to feed an army. Miss Rhodie had the table set with her best china and linens.

I looked at Nola. "I feel shabby," I whispered to her. We wore our church dresses, but they were faded second-hand garments. Daddy and Dewey had gone to extra trouble to spruce up.

Miss Rhodie smiled at Daddy.

"Jim, you sit at the head of the table, and you children can take a seat where you like."

"How did you do all this?" I asked her. Even my bashfulness didn't curb my appetite for the pork, redeye gravy, green beans, mashed potatoes, and sliced tomatoes.

"Oh, Ella, dear, Lethie did most of this. Isn't she something?" she said as Lethie came out of the kitchen with a tray of hot bread.

Daddy had taught us how to be proper, but Dewey began to wolf down his food like a wild animal.

"Son! Son!" Daddy said.

I watched Miss Rhodie and copied her when she picked up her eating utensils.

Miss Rhodie patted her mouth with her napkin. "Jim, what do you think about going into town tomorrow? We'll get material for some new clothes."

"Nola, that okay with you?" Daddy said. But Nola continued to pick at her food and stare down at her plate.

"I don't need any new clothes," she said.

"Yes, you do too!" I said.

Nola stood up and looked at Miss Rhodie.

"You can just take your dad-burned idea and throw it outside," she said. Then she ran to the stairs and disappeared.

Daddy's face turned red and angry. When he got mad, his blue eyes turned steel gray like a sharp knife.

"Eat your supper," he said turning to the boys and me. "I'll see to Nola." He stood up.

"It's all right, Jim," Miss Rhodie intervened, picking up her napkin to pat her mouth.

"No, it's not all right, Rhodie. She's coming back to the table, and she's going to show her elders some respect for a change."

With that, he left for a few minutes and came back with Nola in tow.

"I apologize, Miss Rhodie," she said meekly.

Nola sat down beside me and picked up her fork again. The table was silent except for the clinking of silverware.

Lethie brought in cake. I thought I would die of pleasure, as we hadn't had food so good since Aunt Leah last cooked Sunday dinner.

I pressed my foot on top of Nola's under the table and stared at her.

"Miss Lethie, Nola and I will help you clear the table," I said. Nola then stepped on my foot under the table and gave me a mean sideways look.

"You younguns is tard after such a long trip. Go sit on the porch with yore daddy," Lethie said with a wonderful toothy grin.

It was already dark, so I asked if we could be excused to our rooms.

"Children, first we need to talk to you about the wedding," Miss Rhodie said.

Everything got quiet except the clatter of the dishes from the kitchen. My heart began to race.

Rhodie walked over to Daddy and stood behind his chair with her hands on his shoulders. Daddy looked straight into our faces.

"We are getting married to Miss Rhodie," he said looking at each child individually as he stood up beside her. "Why don't you tell Miss Rhodie how happy you are that she's getting married to us?"

"Congratulations, Miss Rhodie," Dewey said.

"Dewey, dear," she said, "I appreciate your words, but it isn't good form to say 'congratulations.' It's proper to say 'best wishes' instead."

"Oh, oh, sure," he stuttered.

McKinley said nothing.

"Best wishes," Nola and I chimed in. "Now, may we be excused?"

We didn't look at Daddy, and Nola tugged at my arm. "Come on, Sister, I'm worn out. Let's go to bed."

As we went into our room, Dewey and McKinley came out of theirs with the musical instruments.

I looked out the window when they all congregated on the porch. Daddy took the guitar and began strumming it softly. On cue Dewey held his bow in the air, tapped his foot in time, and began playing. Then, McKinley joined in. As we got ready for bed, the music wafted up through our open window. Those sad, lonesome songs still touched my heart and I wished Mama was sitting where Miss Rhodie was.

Later, when the boys came upstairs, Miss Rhodie and Daddy talked quietly. The cool breeze smelled fresh coming through the window. Though it was wonderful, I still felt like a little girl a long way from home.

"Stick your head out the window and thank Miss Rhodie for the nice dinner," I sniffled to Nola as I turned down our bed. She looked at my face and saw my red eyes. She turned abruptly to the window.

"Thank you for dinner, Miss Rhodie," she called out the window.

"Oh, you're welcome, dear," Miss Rhodie said without looking up.

Nola turned to me and said, "I'm sad too, Sister. But anyway, Miss Rhodie's got a big fanny!"

Now, Miss Rhodie's robust bottom had nothing to do with anything. That's why my tears stopped and I began giggling. Nola picked up the signal, and we were both out of control. We were making crazy faces at each other and dancing around.

"Girls, quiet down up there!" Daddy shouted.

"Yes sir!" Nola said and stuck out her fanny at me. We got tickled again.

"With this good food, we might get to look just like Miss Rhodie," I said and stuck my own out, laughing hard again.

Daddy threatened to come up and get us back in line, so we stifled our giggles. Nola got into bed first and was asleep before I got my gown on.

When I drifted off, I felt a pang of guilt for making fun of Miss Rhodie. Mama wouldn't have liked that.

CHAPTER 28

THE WEDDING

The next morning everyone got ready for our trip to town. Rhodie and Daddy rode in the car, and the boys loaded us in our wagon.

Daddy took the boys to a tailor shop. He said it wouldn't take them long to get their purchases. I got the impression men hated to shop, but time would tell.

"We'll go to the dry goods store and find material for new dresses," Miss Rhodie told us. As much as I didn't want to like Miss Rhodie, I sensed she was at least trying to be friendly.

"Are these dresses for the wedding?" Nola asked with a note of sarcasm in her voice.

"Absolutely," she said. "I know you need something new to wear. Your father is like most men; he doesn't realize that women need something pretty to wear at special times."

Daddy and the boys finished their shopping before we had hardly begun.

"I got the suits all lined up with the tailor," Daddy said, "and they'll be ready in a few days."

It took all morning to pick out the right material. We gathered up thread, lace, buttons, ribbons, and several yards of cloth. Miss

Rhodie chose the colors for us because she said she had a sense of fashion. Daddy and the boys stood outside waiting on us, standing on one foot and then the other and looking impatient.

Miss Rhodie wasn't about to be rushed, though, and I could see she had a mind of her own.

"Take your time, girls," she said. "We need to get just exactly what you want, or you won't wear it. Money doesn't grow on trees."

Nola and I were tongue-tied. It seemed odd shopping with a perfect stranger.

"You're two pretty girls," Rhodie said, appearing not to notice our shyness. "You just need some help enhancing what nature gave you."

Maybe I was wrong about Miss Rhodie. What she had just said sounded hopeful.

While we were shopping for material, Daddy and the boys picked out new hats and store-bought shirts.

Daddy smiled at Rhodie. "Did you get the gals fixed up?"

"Sure did," she said and slid her hand into Daddy's. Miss Rhodie's usually stern face softened when Daddy was around.

When we finally got home, Lethie and Miss Rhodie began taking measurements.

I was embarrassed. I felt awkward undressing in front of strangers.

"Turn around, Ella; let's see, you're not much taller than a june bug." Lethie laughed. "We won't be wasting much cloth on you."

I relaxed then. Lethie was fun.

"Are you doing the sewing?" I asked her.

"Yes ma'am," Lethie said. "I'm the fastest seamstress this side of the Mississippi. But you can help with small stitch work that you're used to doing."

By evening Lethie had begun cutting out the dresses; even Nola looked excited.

When Daddy and Miss Rhodie went out to the porch, he asked us to come also. "It's time we all sit down and talk about what's to come," said Daddy.

"All I want to know," Nola said with her perky little nose in the air, "is how did you two get to know each other?"

"Miss Rhodie and I care about each other and about you," Daddy said. "That's all you need to know right now."

I thought back to my dream last night and my short visit with Mama. I wondered if Mama was wishing she was still here and Rhodie wasn't. But the moment passed, and Miss Rhodie began talking about the material she had picked out for us. We never did really have that conversation Daddy started.

Lethie made our dresses within the week and had us try them on for a fitting.

"Ummm, ummm, don't you look cute!" she said, looking at us and standing back, holding her head first to one side and then the other.

My dress was royal-blue velvet with a white lace collar, and Nola's was dark-green velvet with a big sash in back. Lethie helped convince Daddy to buy us some new Mary Jane shoes and stockings.

When she finished making Miss Rhodie's wedding dress and her own as well, she told everyone to do a dress rehearsal.

"If we model, you have to show off your dress too," I told her laughing.

"Fine with me, honeys. Lethie like nothing better than to wear good togs," she said.

We all assembled in the parlor, and Lethie walked down the stairs turning back and forth, smiling that toothy grin.

"Ummn, ummn," she said, "we need a wedding every week around here. It makes me feel brand-new to wear fine clothes."

Dewey tried on his new suit and kept looking at himself in the mirror. He slicked back his hair with bear grease, which was an oily concoction he said he invented. McKinley put his fine clothes on, but he didn't model them like Dewey.

"I'm not modeling anything. I'm not sold on myself like my little bud is," he said, pointing to Dewey playfully.

"What do you think, Rhodie? Do they look fine enough for a wedding?" Daddy asked proudly, smiling at her. She nodded yes, but she seemed distracted.

Daddy looked at us front and back and had us turn around in front of him several times. "Rhodie, don't you think these children could go to the King's ball, as handsome as they look?" he said, emphasizing his desire for her approval.

"Yes, dear, they look nice. Now, you children go upstairs and hang your clothes up so they don't get soiled."

"I think our queen for the day needs to model her dress!" he said.

Rhodie smiled modestly. "Oh, Jim, that's not in good taste."

"I thought it was bad luck for a bride to show her dress before the wedding," Nola said.

"That's just hearsay, Nola," said Miss Rhodie. "Besides, I'm not of the age to have a wedding gown, just a nice dress."

"How old are you?" Nola asked.

"Nola!" Daddy said. "One thing you never do is ask a woman her age!"

Rhodie broke in, smiling, "How old do you think I am, Nola?"

"Sixty?" Nola inquired.

Daddy started laughing and couldn't get control of himself.

Miss Rhodie did not laugh. Instead, she said she was going to her room to get some things done. After all, she was the only one working on the wedding and carrying the entire load.

I thought Daddy would follow her, but instead he stayed seated.

"Children, it's a trying time for Miss Rhodie, getting everything ready for the wedding and trying to see to you children. Just let her go stew for a while, and she'll get over it."

"And you, young lady," he said to Nola, "better not ask a woman her age again."

He winked at her and said, "By the way, Miss Rhodie is thirty-nine."

Then he went to his room and had a little nap while Miss Rhodie got right with the world again.

Nola and I tossed and turned the whole night before the wedding. We were going to a big hotel in the city to see Daddy and Miss Rhodie get married. We would be wearing our prettiest dresses. I shivered with excitement thinking about it.

Miss Rhodie was a Fundamentalist, so she said she would arrange for her preacher to officiate. She didn't have many friends except from church to invite. I could see why, but it wasn't up to me to tell her she was somewhat on the snooty side.

Daddy took Nola and me to the church. We tried to be very ladylike, and it was easy in our new dresses. I kept looking at my Mary Janes thinking how spiffy my feet looked.

The boys drove Miss Rhodie and Lethie in Her Majesty. We wouldn't get to see the bride until the wedding.

We were intrigued with all the activity. We all fought over the privilege of sitting by Lethie, and finally Nola and I sat on each side of her. Dewey had trouble keeping still, and McKinley gave him mean looks.

Miss Rhodie's lacy beige charmeuse dress was way too tight. She had complained to Lethie that she had tried her best at reducing, but it was in her family to be large in the hips.

"Sometime it do run in de family, Miss Rhodie, but you just fine, Rhodie, just fine," Lethie would say in an endearing tone.

Daddy looked tired, but very handsome for his age. He stood beside the minister as Miss Rhodie came down the aisle with McKinley on one side of her and Dewey on the other. Lethie squeezed our hands and smiled when she saw our brothers giving away the bride.

At the end of the ceremony the preacher said to Daddy, "You may kiss the bride." The small crowd attending started applauding after the kiss and Lethie hugged Nola and me where we were seated in our pew. It was all so beautiful and exciting.

After the service punch and cake were served. Miss Rhodie and Daddy looked like they were both in a daze as they greeted guests in the receiving line. Finally, everyone sat down at lovely tables to eat their cake and punch.

Daddy came over to us finally and said, "We're all married to Miss Rhodie now. Let's please be nice to her, all right?"

We all told him yes sir.

Then Daddy shocked us.

"Miss Rhodie and I will be staying at the hotel tonight. You'll be going home with Lethie. Y'all run along now and have sweet dreams."

When we left the reception Nola said, "Why can't we stay at the hotel tonight too? Daddy never took *us* to a hotel."

"They need time to be alone and talk," Lethie said. "They starting a new life together, and they got to make plans."

"I'm gonna live in a place like that some day," said Nola. "With shiny floors and pretty pictures on the wall and velvet furniture."

"With your red dress on and your red hat and red shoes?" I asked deadpan serious.

"Shush, Sister! I mean it!" Nola said.

"Ella, stop playing them practical jokes on you little sister," Lethie said. "She don't understand."

"Okay, then, she needs to smarten up," I said.

"Come, little ladies, let me get you in bed. It's been a tiring day," Lethie said.

"I wonder if Daddy's all right. I don't like him stuck there in that old hotel without us," Nola said.

"He be fine, honey," Lethie said. "They be home not tomorrow, but the next tomorrow."

"It sure was a nice party, wasn't it, Lethie?" I said. "We like the dresses you made."

"I be making you a wedding dress one of these days," she said.

"Well, maybe," I mumbled as I drifted off to sleep thinking about Troy Clark.

CHAPTER 29
LITTLE ROCK LIVING

Daddy went back to work in January. Miss Rhodie arranged for us all to go to school in Little Rock. We all felt lost when we went to our new classrooms as we were separated for the first time into individual grades. Also, we felt like country bumpkins compared to the city slickers in Little Rock. Although Pine Bluff was a sizeable modern town, it was filled with friendly people. Little Rock was new to us, and we were among strangers who were already familiar with each other. We felt left out.

Miss Rhodie had a buggy and a driver who wanted to take us every day, but we were too embarrassed and backward to ride in it. Instead, we got up early enough to walk. Dewey was a very social boy, so he soon had friends, but Nola and I kept to ourselves.

McKinley was blue a lot of the time. He missed his friends back home, so Daddy and Miss Rhodie thought up a project for him. Hard work cures an idle mind, they said.

"McKinley, I want you to build a garage for the car," Miss Rhodie said.

He said he had no clue as to how to start, but Miss Rhodie had an answer to that. She had farmhands who were able carpenters. So McKinley began slowly, and with the help of the other men, erected a fine building, painted it nest egg blue, and drove the car into it.

It was a proud day when Daddy came home from the railroad and saw McKinley's achievement. Daddy and Rhodie were smiling at each other. and McKinley looked like my brother again. The hard work had paid off, and he had come to life again.

"Your next project, McKinley, is to teach Miss Rhodie to drive," Daddy said.

"Oh, Jim, no!" she said. "I'd be afraid."

"McKinley can teach you real easy-like, and you'll do just fine."

McKinley looked skeptical. It wasn't every day that a woman drove a car. In fact I had never seen a woman drive a car. But Daddy said McKinley needed the job, and Miss Rhodie needed to learn how to drive.

Lethie stood on the porch grinning big, listening to the talk about the new driver.

"One day all you ladies be driving a car," she said, pointing her finger at Nola and me.

"Then we'll teach you!" I said.

"Baby, too much water gone under the bridge for Lethie to learn how to drive," she said. She looked off in the distance, and her smile faded away.

"What's wrong, Lethie?" Nola said.

"Just watching you two make me think about my own baby girl. She die last spring."

"What happened to her?" I asked.

"She borned wid a heart problem, and she lasted out till her poor little heart wouldn't beat no more."

I put my arms around her soft middle and stayed there a minute.

"What was her name?"

"Her name be Evvie," she said sadly.

"I'm sorry, Lethie. I know how you feel. We lost our real mama."

"I guess de Lord know what he doing, and his world is turning like he see fit."

"Did Evvie go to our school?" Nola asked.

"No, baby. My kind of children don't get to go to school very much, and if they do, they go to the colored schools."

"Why?" Nola asked.

"People like me just be maids and farm workers, honey," Lethie said. "Someday things might be different in your lifetime, but not mine."

"Maids and farmers are just as important as anybody else," I said.

"We just the wrong color," she said and looked away.

"Oh, I think we white folks may be the wrong color if we keep some of the children from going to school," I said.

"Well, I'm definitely going to drive. And it's going to be a red car," said Nola, changing the subject.

"There's no such thing as a red car," I said. "They're all black."

"I'll get McKinley to paint it red," she said.

"And you'll have on your red hat and your red dress and your red shoes?" I asked.

"Shush, Ella! Don't remind me of that awful day in church!" she said.

Later that evening I went to the porch to talk to McKinley.

"McKinley, did you know that white people don't go to colored schools, and colored people don't go to white schools?" I asked.

"Yes," he said, "but Pine Bluff was different from most towns. Their school for colored people has outranked many a white man's school. I know it's a lot better than that one-room schoolhouse we were in."

"When you go to the army, won't there be colored soldiers too?" I asked.

"I don't really know," he said, "but I imagine they're in France fighting just like anyone else."

"Then, why doesn't everybody go to school together? Lethie said her kind of children in this part of the country don't always get to go to school."

"Too poor. Too broken down," he said and turned away.

The way he said it made me know he was describing himself. He looked at me helplessly, and that's when I blew my stack.

"Just wake up, McKinley," I said. "You're acting like a dead person."

I ran inside. Lethie had been standing by the door listening.

"Don't be too hard on your brother, baby," she said. "He feel bad for leaving his school and friends. He don't seem to adjust like you and Nola and Dewey is."

"He needs to get hold of himself," I said, not cutting him any slack.

"Just be patient," she said, patting me on the back. "He'll come back around to us."

CHAPTER 30
VISITING CHARLIE WRIGHT

One day while Daddy was home, Dewey asked if he would take us to the asylum to see Charlie Wright.

"Son, I don't know if that is a good place for children," he said.

"Come on, Daddy. I'm going to be a doctor. I understand about sick people."

"Let me think about it," Daddy said, his way of ending the subject. But Dewey kept on.

"Daddy, he saved Nola's life. Don't we owe Charlie a visit?"

"I want to see him too," Nola said quietly.

"Take us all over there, Daddy. We like Charlie," I said.

So it was on Saturday that we loaded up Her Majesty and drove over to the asylum. Miss Rhodie complained of a headache and said she didn't see why we wanted to visit someone in an asylum. It brought back to mind the time I hurt Charlie's feelings about his sickness.

The big red brick building sat at the top of a hill, isolated from the rest of the town. There were a few scrawny trees around it, but that was all. Above the front entrance were the words Arkansas Lunatic Asylum.

We sat in the car, and Daddy went inside to find Charlie.

"Miss Rhodie needs to be in here herself," said Nola.

"You're being mean," I said.

"She *is* nervous," said Nola. "She only has a good face when Daddy comes around. All other times she's picking on one of us."

"Let's give her the benefit of the doubt," said McKinley.

"Then, I doubt," said Nola.

We got out stretching our legs. Several cars were parked harum-scarum beside the building along with a few wagons. I guessed that mental illness didn't pick its families, be they rich or poor. Finally, Daddy came out.

"Now, children, I want you to keep your thoughts to yourself and not talk when we go in. There are a lot of people sitting in the hallways who aren't well. Just mind your own business till the nurse brings Charlie out."

We stepped inside the door. The waiting room was well lit and bare of furniture. We sat on a hard bench waiting for Daddy to bring Charlie to us.

Finally, they appeared.

"You got any biscuits?" he asked me, giggling. His eyes belied any happiness in his laugh. They were empty.

"No, I didn't bring any," I said weakly.

"Let's go outside for a visit, Charlie," Daddy said.

Charlie had his tobacco and papers. I was surprised the doctors let him smoke, but he said they would let him in the courtyard.

"How's the world treating you, Charlie?" Dewey said.

"Well, now," he began slowly, pausing as he rolled a cigarette and lit it. "I've had a time of it. They give me hot baths and ice baths to calm my nerves, but it's not helping much. The food ain't no good either."

"Are the doctors good to you?" Dewey asked.

"They try," he said. "But when somebody gets too loud they take them off somewhere to a dark place to calm down."

"Ever happened to you, Charlie?" McKinley said.

"Once," Charlie said, inhaling his Bull Durham. He blew four smoke rings into the air as if we weren't there.

"Let's talk about something happy," Daddy said. "Did you know we have moved to Little Rock and got married to a nice lady named Rhodie?"

"Sure enough?" Charlie said. "Well, Jimbo, that's good news. Can I come home with you?"

Oops, I thought. That was going too far.

"They won't let us take you home," Daddy said. "But we'll come see you every once in a while until you get to go to your own home. Do you see your mama and daddy very often?"

"Not too," he said. "Well, I better go. Bye," Charlie said and abruptly got up and walked back into the building.

We all looked at each other.

"Well, all righty," Daddy said in a confused tone of voice. "That ended our visit. Guess it's time we head back to the farm."

Daddy left for work in the next few days, and McKinley began teaching Miss Rhodie to drive. She was totally frantic in these episodes. She would get into the driver's seat, rev up the engine, and try to chug off in leaps and dives and sputters. She pretended to us it was part of the plan, but McKinley told us she was ruining Her Majesty.

She practiced backing Her Majesty out of the garage and pulling it back in. She practiced driving down the road and driving back. She practiced shifting gears but got mixed up with first gear and reverse.

"Miss Rhodie, you're stripping the gears!" McKinley would yell.

"Then you drive it yourself, young man," she'd say and get out of the car, huffing back to the house.

"You're never going to get this until you listen to what I'm trying to tell you," McKinley would say.

"That's the last time I'm getting in that car," she'd say. But the next day, she'd be right back in the driver's seat, grinding the gears again.

Life had been easy for Miss Rhodie until we came along. That was obvious. But none of us had the bravado to ask her questions about what made her tick.

One Saturday after we had done our shopping, I sat down with Miss Rhodie. She was in a particularly good mood.

"How long have you lived on this farm?" I asked.

"It goes back two generations," she said. "My grandfather came to Arkansas while the savages were still roaming. He began buying up acreage until he had a right good-sized piece of property."

"Did your grandfather come from another country?" I asked, wondering who the savages were.

"Oh yes, Ella. He came from Germany and eventually brought his brothers and sisters over. He thought Arkansas was the Garden of Eden."

"It is mighty beautiful." I said. "How do you buy land?"

"You save your money like my grandfather did, and you'll be able to help several generations with what you buy," she said, pleased with her own words.

I wished McKinley could hear this. He was the one who needed to buy land. All I wanted to do was become a singer.

"How did you and Daddy meet?" I asked.

"I took a train trip to Oklahoma," she said. "I have a cousin there. Your daddy was working on the train when we met. We felt like we were right for each other at first meeting."

I felt myself blushing all the way to my toes.

"Did you know about us?" I asked.

"Right off, your daddy began telling me about each of you."

"Now, you don't have any children, right?" I said.

She smiled. "Some people have called me an old maid. If you don't get married before you're twenty, that's what a girl is called in these parts," she said.

"An old maid isn't such a bad thing to be." I laughed. "I may be one if I'm a singer."

"You've got the voice for it," she said to my surprise. "But women can't be independent without wealth in their family."

"I'll make my own money," I said. "I'm going to sing on the radio."

"That's a long time from now, Ella. Right now you need to go up and work on your embroidery. I'm going to get Lethie to show you how to do needlepoint too one of these days. Girls do need a genteel hobby."

"Genteel?" I asked.

"That's a word for people with refinement. I'm going to help you acquire the right habits to become genteel."

All I wanted to do was get out of there. I stared out the window and noticed Nola and Dewey playing kick the can, and I was jealous. I felt too old to do that and too young to have the conversation I'd just had. But then, I remembered Miss Rhodie's trip to Oklahoma.

"Where does your cousin live in Oklahoma?" I asked.

"Tulsa," she said quietly.

"Did Daddy go to see my brother there?" I asked.

"You need to talk to your daddy about Daniel," she said. "It isn't my place."

Now wait a minute. I hadn't said the name Daniel to her. Before I could ask another question, Miss Rhodie had rushed into her bedroom, closing the door behind her.

The sun had gone down, and it was my favorite time of day. I walked outside and saw Dewey chasing Nola around the yard with a cricket.

"Make him stop, Sister!" Nola whined and ran to me for cover.
Dewey was jumping around laughing his head off.

"She's just a sissy," he said, still laughing. "No bigger than a
peanut and scared of a little old frog."

"Shut up!" Nola yelled.

Miss Rhodie opened the screen door and looked out.

"Young man, if you keep that up, I'm going to get a switch.
Now, leave the girls alone!"

He looked at her but didn't say yes ma'am. He slid past her,
almost knocking her over.

Miss Rhodie came outside, letting the door slam behind her.
She furiously marched over to the small tree nearest the porch,
pulled off a switch, and went in after Dewey. I was scared because
I hadn't known Miss Rhodie had a temper that bad. Nola and I
stood together and listened.

Whack! Whack! Whack! She was really busting him. It hurt my
heart to think my brother was getting whipped, especially by an
outsider. She didn't know anything about us, yet she took it upon
herself to punish Dewey for just being a kid. I heard him begging
for her to stop, but he didn't cry. I knew that iron will of his; he
wouldn't let Miss Rhodie see him as a weakling. Finally, she came
to the door.

"Get in the house, and go to bed, girls. This has been a long
day," she said and sighed.

"Just wait till I tell Daddy," Nola said. "He wouldn't want you
hurting Dewey."

She turned around and pointed her finger at Nola. "Don't start
it, or you'll get a whipping too, Nola. I've had about enough of your
back talk."

I glanced at Nola, and she didn't budge. Lethie came around
the corner and saved us both from the fiery furnace.

"Come on girls. I'll help you get into your gowns. Off to bed,"
she said, but her toothy grin was missing.

Nola and I pulled the fresh sheets down on our bed. They smelled sweet from their day hanging in the sun. It wasn't our musty covers from our bed in Pine Bluff, and I knew this was a better and more genteel way of life. But oh, how I wanted that musty-smelling house back and Miss Rhodie gone.

Sometime in the middle of the night, Dewey slipped into our room and woke me.

"Start getting your things together tomorrow, but don't let her see you. We're going to run away from here where she can't find us."

CHAPTER 31

NEW DRIVER

The boys had made a plan. McKinley would start secretly getting the wagon in good shape. Then, at the right time in the next few days, we would put our belongings in it and travel to a safe place. Nola wanted to bring Lethie, but Dewey said that would be a bad arrangement.

Daddy would be at work for two more weeks. We would have to walk the line to keep Miss Rhodie from getting mad again. Then, when no one was looking, the four of us would escape with plenty of food and enough money to get to our unknown destination.

It wasn't to be, though, because Miss Rhodie decided to put a monkey wrench in our plans. She resolved to be a proficient driver by Daddy's return, so McKinley was enlisted into her service every day after school. The two of them went up and down the road several times with Miss Rhodie clutching and braking and making wide turns in the road. It took several days, but finally, McKinley pronounced her ready for a solo drive. We all sat on the porch watching the new driver emerge.

"Come with me, Lethie!" she said, practicing backing up to the house. Lethie's eyes widened, but she kept on smiling and walked to the car. She got in, and the two women rode off down the road bouncing and jostling.

"Her Majesty can go faster than five miles an hour!" Dewey yelled. "Speed up!"

Miss Rhodie didn't hear him, because she and Lethie were both concentrating on the road ahead. Finally, about an hour later, when we thought they had driven to Tulsa or somewhere else far away, they sputtered back.

When they came to the front of the garage, Miss Rhodie stopped the car.

"Drive it on in," McKinley said, pointing to the garage. "You need the practice."

"I don't think I can fit it in there!" she said.

McKinley cranked the car for her again, and she got back in. She looked to the right and then the left to assure she could squeeze Her Majesty in. She gave it some gas, and the car shot out suddenly as if it were driving itself. Boom! Boards began falling off as if the garage had been shot down.

Miss Rhodie and Lethie came out from the back of the garage shrieking and crying.

"Oh Lordy, I couldn't get my foot on the brake!" Miss Rhodie said, sobbing.

"Tha's all right, Miss Rhodie," said Lethie. "You did yo' best. We won't be doin' that no more."

McKinley walked to the site of the calamity. Then he turned to Miss Rhodie and put his hand on her shoulder.

"You didn't mean to, Rhodie. Stop crying now," he said softly.

She jerked away from McKinley and ran up the steps.

"You should have known better than to make me drive through that building. It was your fault, not mine, you lazy moocher!"

McKinley had not been called names before, and it seemed to knock the breath out of him. He stood for a moment looking at the damage and walked off.

"Come on, Dew, let's at least see what can be salvaged out of this," he mumbled, not looking at Rhodie now at the front door of the house.

Dewey and McKinley were still working when the rest of the house was fast asleep. The next morning when I walked outside with my coffee milk, it was all still a disaster.

Splintered and broken boards were all over the place. One wall was missing. The car was all streaked up where the paint had come off. Miss Rhodie came out walking like a zombie.

"No one seemed to care if I got hurt or not," she said. "And Lethie, where is she this morning? No breakfast cooking or anything done."

Lethie came out of the house looking pale.

"Oh my Lordy! I got white knuckles from that drive, Miss Rhodie. You poor thing...you couldn't help it. You tried yore best."

"People," she said quietly to Lethie and me, "please straighten up the mess for me. I've driven my last time."

She never mentioned the incident again, and she never drove again as long as I knew her.

CHAPTER 32
LIFE GONE AWRY

After Miss Rhodie was humbled, life took a turn. We settled into a routine of living day-to-day, feeling somehow empowered.

Daddy and Miss Rhodie developed one of those relationships that relied on disputing each other's word and grumbling. If Daddy said today was Sunday, Miss Rhodie would say it was Monday. Daddy began staying at work more days than usual, which I now realize was probably to get away from the fussing. But I thought he had stopped liking us, his very own flesh and blood, because he didn't even talk to us anymore.

When I asked Lethie what was wrong with Daddy, she said he stayed away so much because he didn't like being criticized.

"Ella, Mr. Smith, he tard when he come in from the railroad. Miss Rhodie, she peck, peck, peck at him, and he swells up like a toad and won't talk."

I knew that we four children were the reason for the feuding. I walked around with a black cloud of guilt over me, but I couldn't have explained it if I tried.

Dewey set Miss Rhodie off with his experiments. He put substances together and left them in the kitchen to mold. Then he would forget about them until a strange odor smelled up the house. Once he cut up onions and garlic, poured milk and vinegar in a glass, and placed the mixture inside a nook in the cabinet. After days the hidden vessel radiated such an odor that Lethie got frantic.

"What dat smell is?" she said as she opened and closed drawers. "Don't smell like no mouse dat died in de wall."

When she got Miss Rhodie in on the search, the elusive container was retrieved.

"Dewey," Miss Rhodie said, "take that mess out by the barn and bury it, glass and all."

"I was just trying to invent medicine," he told her.

"And what would this horrible concoction cure?" Miss Rhodie said, hands on her hips.

"I'm looking for a cure for stomach problems," he told her, but she didn't buy it.

"You don't have stomach problems," she said. "What's the point?"

"Lots of people do have stomach problems, and I'm going to invent medicine to cure them."

Miss Rhodie pulled back a strand of hair that had gotten in her eye and pinned it back with a hairpin.

"Dewey, that's a noble thought, but a young Arkansas boy like you is not going to formulate anything but trouble."

"Just you wait and see," he said with his sweetest smile. "I'm going to be a doctor someday, and you might need me to help you."

"Oh, pshaw," she said. "That's a bunch of bosh."

"That's swearing, Miss Rhodie," Nola said.

"Nola! The insolence and disrespect you show for your elders is intolerable!" Miss Rhodie said.

Nola looked up at her and stunned us all again. "Well, that was a mouthful. What does it mean?" she said.

I pinched Nola on the backside and hurried her outside.

"Nola, can't you keep your mouth shut? Miss Rhodie is gonna switch you if you don't shush."

"What do I care what she thinks? She's not my mama," Nola said.

Miss Rhodie ran out to Nola with fire in her eyes.

"You're not my daughter either, but you sure don't mind living in my home, now do you?"

"I do too mind!" Nola yelled.

With that, Miss Rhodie grabbed Nola by her two arms and began to pull her. Nola, little and proud, was not going down without a fight. She struggled and twisted, and Miss Rhodie held tighter and tighter. Nola landed on the ground, and Miss Rhodie, sweating and furious, dragged her through a patch of stickers and weeds. Over and over she pulled her back and forth.

"She's hurt!" I screamed, seeing blood oozing from her legs.

"Well, there," said Miss Rhodie, stopping to take a deep breath. "Now, you know you don't talk back to me."

"No ma'am," Nola said weakly.

"Take her in, and have Lethie clean her up," Miss Rhodie said, turning to go in to the house. "Never a word of this to your father or you'll be in for the same thing."

McKinley was silent. He picked up Nola and carried her up the stairs and into our room. Dewey put water on to heat and brought it up, and the three of us cleaned her up.

"Where's Lethie?" I asked Dewey.

"Already in her room asleep," he said, dabbing alcohol on the scratches.

McKinley found tweezers and picked stickers out of Nola's feet and legs. Though she flinched, Nola was too beaten down to move.

"I give up for tonight, but I'm not quitting," she said, closing her eyes. "Will you sing to me, Ella?"

I began to hum very low so Miss Rhodie wouldn't hear. Nola and I got into bed, and the boys made pallets beside us. I kept humming. The hurt was too deep in any of us to talk. We all slept together that night, protecting our spirits as we had done so many times after Mama died. Once again, I felt like a little girl a long way from home.

CHAPTER 33

ESCAPING

We had to get away from Miss Rhodie, especially Nola. We would have to escape when Miss Rhodie and Lethie were occupied with something else and while Daddy was away. We would take the wagon and mules because they were already ours, and that wouldn't be stealing. Daddy didn't use the wagon anymore, and the mules had seen better days.

"Let's go to Tulsa and find little Daniel," I said.

"Don't know anything about Oklahoma, Sister," said McKinley. "We better go to parts we know about."

"Let's just go home," said Dewey. "We can write Daddy a letter and tell him where we'll be. He'll understand if we explain it."

"Oh, Daddy doesn't care about us anyway," Nola said.

I wrote to Kit and told her about our plan to run away. She wrote back and promised not to tell—that is, unless we failed to keep in touch. That would mean we were in trouble and needed help.

I began daydreaming about Pine Bluff and eating Aunt Leah's cooking and messing around with Kit.

"The first thing I'm going to do is find Miss Bonner so she can tell us about little Daniel," I told Nola.

"Maybe Daddy can get unhitched from Rhodie and we can all marry Miss Bonner," she said.

"If he gets unhitched, I don't think he'll make the mistake of marrying again," Dewey said.

"Let's just keep focused on pulling this off," said McKinley.

"We're all in this together," said Dewey. "Might as well make it an adventure."

As good fortune would have it, Miss Rhodie decided to take the train to see her cousin in Oklahoma.

"This is perfect," Dewey said. "After Rhodie leaves, we can pack up the wagon and leave when school lets out one day."

"Let's take Lethie," I said. "She would be happy going with us."

"Bad idea, Sister. If we asked her, she'd refuse to go, and then she'd run right out and tell Rhodie," McKinley said. "Let's stick to our plan."

On the morning of the big day, we finished placing our clothes and food into the wagon. Since Miss Rhodie was gone, Nola and I wore our good dresses and our latest Mary Janes just to celebrate.

"Have a good day, honeys," said Lethie waving and smiling big.

"Yes, ma'am!" we said and saluted. "You have a good one too."

I ran back and gave her an extra big hug.

As we walked down the road, I looked back at the house and saw Lethie still standing in the door.

"Bye, Lethie! See ya later!" I yelled. But I was certain I would never see this angel again.

We met Dewey after school at the back of the building.

"Come on," he said. "McKinley left school early and is down the road waiting for us."

Nola and I walked along together with our heads down. I felt unsettled about being deceitful. I envisioned Lethie's reaction when we didn't show up after school. I saw Daddy's face in my mind, worried and inconsolable.

It was hot and muggy, and our clothes clung to us. When we got to the wagon, McKinley stepped down and helped us in. The wagon was packed with our clothes, food, water, and hay for the mules to eat.

"It's four o'clock," Dewey said, looking at his pocket watch. "If we can get two or three hours of travel in before dark, we'll be way down the road."

"Did you leave Daddy a letter?" I asked.

"Yep," McKinley said. "Explained we wanted to go back home and that we felt like we were in Miss Rhodie's way."

"What about Lethie? Did you leave her a letter too?" Nola asked.

"I left her a note," said McKinley.

Dewey climbed in the back and reached for Nola and me. McKinley had put some pillows there for us to sit on. It was a miracle and not like our brother. Then he went up front with McKinley, and they talked about what kind of musical gigs they could get in the Pine Bluff area.

"Let's go by and see Charlie," Nola said.

"Heard his folks already came and took him back home. We'll go see him in Pine Bluff," McKinley said.

Our mules were getting old and clopped along at a snail's pace. We were used to riding in Her Majesty going as fast as twenty miles an hour, and it was hard to stay patient.

Miss Rhodie's farm was on the southeast edge of town, and we figured we could get six miles away to Wrightsville by dark. The ride was bumpy, and Dewey had to hop off the wagon several times to move rocks from the road.

The pine trees were thick along the dirt road, and we looked up at the many hills with big rocks jutting out. I imagined Indians had once lived in those hills. The sun was shining through the trees like a lamplight flickering on glass. As we got closer to Wrightsville, shadows began to fall against the road in slanted lines.

"Don't you think it's about time to stop for the night?" asked Dewey.

McKinley nodded. "There's a creek up the way," he said. "We'll stop off there and find a good clearing."

Finding a good clearing in Arkansas is more easily said than done. Trees loom thickly everywhere. But McKinley found a place that satisfied him and went to the creek side to build a fire.

"Where's the outhouse?" Nola whispered to me. "I need to tinkle."

"We'll have to go over in those bushes," I said. "We better go now before it gets dark and the critters come out."

When we got back up to camp, the smell of smoke was drifting into the fresh air. Dewey tied up the mules to a tree and fed them. McKinley put an iron skillet on the fire and laid slices of salt pork in it. As it sizzled, Dewey brought out some of Lethie's biscuits. Nola and I found the tin plates and cups and spread one of Mama's quilts on the ground.

The fire flickered and spit off mother-in-law sparks, as Daddy called them. It reminded me of our fireplace in Pine Bluff.

With our stomachs full and the excitement dying down, we decided to turn in for the night.

"You girls sleep in the wagon," McKinley said. "The men will sleep on the ground."

"Men?" Nola said. "Where are the men?"

McKinley furrowed his eyebrows. "Just get in the wagon and go to sleep."

Nola and I climbed up into the wagon and took our Mary Janes off.

"Ooooo, that feels good," I said as I stretched out my feet.

"Nighty night, sleep tight, and don't let the bed bugs bite," said Dewey like he was Daddy.

"Nite," we said in unison.

It was dark, and the leaves on the trees were moving like they were talking to each other. Nola and I snuggled so we wouldn't be afraid. It had been a day to end all days.

I woke in the night with a terrible smell in my nostrils.

"Dewey! There's a skunk around here!"

The boys hopped up looking for their guns.

"Careful there, Dewey," McKinley said. "Don't shoot me!" he said looking at Dewey, who was swinging his gun around like a loose cannon.

He lit the lantern, and the skunk scampered away spraying the wagon as he passed by.

"Pew-ee!" said Nola, waking up. "I smell a skunk!"

"Just go back to sleep; it's already gone," said McKinley.

But no one went back to sleep, and finally McKinley said it was 4:00 a.m. according to his pocket watch, and we were going to head down the road.

It took about an hour to get out of the thicket of woods. We could see dawn was coming, so McKinley stopped the team and built a fire.

"Got to have some coffee," he said. "Can't go on without some coffee."

"Me too," Nola said, and she meant it. Coffee milk was the first thing we drank every morning, and Miss Rhodie had given up stopping us.

The fire felt good, as we were all chilled to the bone. Dewey sat the coffee on the fire, and it began bubbling.

Suddenly, from nowhere, a blast of thunder shattered the still morning.

"Better hurry," Dewey said. "It's going to rain."

"That's all we need—to be trying to drive this old wagon down muddy roads," said McKinley.

Dewey scrambled around picking up things and throwing them into the wagon. McKinley poured salt on the fire, and the blazing flames settled to a slow burn.

"We'll drive across the road and get under that grove of trees," said McKinley. "Shouldn't get too wet over there."

"Sister, put everything under that tarp," Dewey said.

It started misting, and I hurried to get everything covered. Something flew out of the wagon, but I couldn't be concerned. It was going to pour down on us if we didn't hurry.

"Giddyup, Jenny," McKinley said and sailed us across the road to a grove of pines.

During the ten-minute downpour, we held the tarp over us to protect our food and clothing. When the rain stopped, McKinley clucked to the mules to get going again, but we were stuck.

Dewey got into the driver's seat while McKinley got behind the wagon and pushed. He finally got one of the tired old wheels out of a rut, and Jenny sailed off with us while McKinley stood there looking confused.

"Whoa, girl," Dewey said, laughing. "Wait on us."

Instead, the team kept going and pulled us squarely off into a trench. McKinley was able to catch up with us then because we were prisoners of the ditch.

The boys tried to lift the wheel that was stuck. McKinley said some bad cuss words that he'd picked up at school, and Dewey repeated him. They were both sweating and giving directions and repeating the bad words.

"Oh, Lordy, help us all," said McKinley pulling out his pocket watch. "It'll take a week or two to get to Pine Bluff at this rate."

He peered down under the wagon. "I think we have a broken axle."

"What does that mean?" I asked.

"Just never mind, Sister; it means the wagon can't go."

"Then, how are we going to run away?" said Nola.

"Be quiet, Nola," Dewey said. "This is only a hiccup in the road of life."

"Stop joking around," said McKinley. "This is serious."

"Let's think this thing out," said Dewey, plastering his hair back with his fingers. "I saw a house down the way. Let me go see if I can get someone to pull us out."

"Was it that big white house way back off the road?" asked McKinley.

"Yep, and it's not too far. In fact, I think I see smoke coming out of the chimney from here."

"You two women straighten out that stuff in the back," Dewey said and giggled. "I'll go up to that house."

"Oh sure, leave us here with the skunky-smelling wagon!" Nola said, not paying attention to Dewey's teasing.

Sitting at a slant in the wagon, we began to straighten everything up.

"Where in thunder is my shoe?" I asked, looking around for my other Mary Jane.

"You must have dropped it out when the wagon took off," said McKinley.

"Will you please, please, please go over there and look for it?" I asked McKinley, almost crying.

He didn't answer but started walking over to the pine grove. In a few minutes, he came back with a patent-leather strap in his hand.

"Something must have taken it off, Sister," he said. "I sure am sorry."

"Sorry, nothing! I need that shoe!" I said and started running toward the place where the wagon had sat.

There I saw my precious Mary Jane, squished by the wagon wheel flatter than a fritter.

"Thanks a lot!" I yelled at McKinley. "Now I have to go barefoot."

He was building another fire and putting on more coffee. That helped a bit to make the day a little brighter.

McKinley unhooked the mules and gave them food and water from our supply.

"Did they get hurt?" I asked.

"Seem to be fine. Mules can take a lot of rough ground."

I looked over at the pathetic wagon. Only a miracle could save it now.

CHAPTER 34

SAINTS OF CALVARY

The miracle showed up in the form of a tall man on a horse, his face weathered from working in the sun.

"So you had an accident," he said. "Yer brother came over to the house and asked me to see about you. He's driving my wagon over."

Sure enough, Dewey rode up on a fine wagon with two huge horses.

"I'm McKinley Smith."

"Glen Porter," he said. "Let's get started. This is cutting into my workday."

Glen wiped the sweat off his face with a handkerchief. "One of you boys take the girls over to the house and come back in the wagon. No sense in them hanging around here getting in the way."

McKinley pulled out the toolbox. "This is all we have: axle grease and a jack."

"Get the tools out of my wagon...it's gonna take all day. Take them gals to the house, and we'll get started."

Nola and I hurried to get into Glen's wagon with our things. Dewey got on the driver's side.

"Haw!" he said to the horses in the same manner he did to the mules. They took off in a mad dash down the road to the big white house with the smoke coming out. The yard was full of children and about a thousand cats.

Nola and I got down from the wagon shyly. I had no shoes, but none of the children I saw wore any either.

"Howdy do, I'm Alma Porter," said a woman wearing a split bonnet and a big checkered apron over her dress. I recognized the material it was made from; I'd seen a sack of flour with the same design in Dalby Brothers Grocery Store.

"How many cats you got?" asked Nola, looking at the yard zoo.

"B'lieve we have about eighteen," she said, spitting snuff into the grass. "Got seven children too."

She turned around and pointed to them.

"Now there's Ruth, that's Esther, over yonder hiding behind the washtub is Titus, this here's James, and the other three are working in the fields for their pa. Tried to get us a band of disciples!" she laughed and spit again into the grass.

Dewey was itching to get away and told Alma he had to get back to our broken wagon.

"Tell Glen to get home by suppertime," she said. "Y'all can eat with us."

"Yes, ma'am," he said and didn't let the gate hit him in the back before he was out of there.

Nola and I stood in the grass not knowing what to do.

"Sorry we're so tousled, but we've been in an accident and I lost a shoe, and everything's a mess…" I said.

I heard something buzzing around my head, and then a bee zeroed in on me and stung my arm before I could move. Ouch!

I folded up into a little bundle and started crying as if I'd been killed.

"Don't you worry none, Miss. I'll fix that bee sting," Alma said.

With that, she took something from her mouth and doctored my arm with it. I saw snuff on my arm through my tears.

"I think I'm gonna throw up," I said.

"Sometimes them old insect stings make you sick at your stomach. Come on, I'll take you in the house."

As she took us inside, Alma looked at us quizzically and said, "You're not by any chance part of the Saints of Calvary, are you?"

"No ma'am," I said. "Daddy said if we ever open a door to one of those people, he's gonna whack us."

"Well, we are Saints of Calvary in this house, and I'm going to teach you the true way of believing."

I gulped and took my foot out of my mouth.

"Sorry if I was rude about your religion," I said weakly.

Alma obviously hadn't been listening, because she shuffled us inside without saying a word. The family and cats followed us. The children looked at us curiously.

"Whatch yo' name, little girl?" asked James.

"I'm Ella and she's Nola," I said pointing to my sister, whose eyes were getting bigger by the second.

"Them names ain't from the Bible, now are they?" asked James.

"Don't think so," I said as I tried to push away a cat who was curling his tail around my leg.

"You don't like cats, do ye, little girl?" James said.

"I do too. I have one at my aunt's house named Callie; we got her for Christmas one year."

"Don't talk about Christmas to my ma and pa," said James. "They told me Jesus was borned on October first, so we don't celebrate Christmas. Don't celebrate birthdays neither. If you study, you'll find out pagans and heathens started that practice."

"Well, everybody's different," I said.

"T'aint so," said James, coming toward me, staring at my neck.

"What are you staring at?" I asked.

"Taking a look at that heathen necklace you got on," he said.

I turned around quickly and let my chain and cross fall into the bodice of my dress so it wouldn't show.

"It's not a heathen necklace," I said, feeling of my necklace. "It's a cross."

Then I took Nola's hand and parted company with James. I led her into the kitchen, where Alma was cooking.

Nola and I sat together in a chair and watched the kids playing. They weren't a rambunctious lot, and I soon found out why.

"It's twelve noon, you'ens. Time to eat dinner."

We followed the children to the table, and everyone took a seat. Alma had Nola and me sit side by side. She was very strict with her children, but not unkind.

"Bow your heads, and let's pray," she said. "God, thank you for this day and all its many blessings. Bless this food to the nourishment of our bodies. Amen."

She passed around a bowl of pinto beans and a platter of fried potatoes. But the best part was a big slice of hot cornbread slathered with butter.

"What are you children doing, off without your mama and papa?" she asked.

I pinched Nola so she wouldn't say anything weird. The least said the better.

"We're going to Pine Bluff. That's our real home," I said.

"That where your family lives?"

"Umm hmm," I said, crossing my fingers because it was only a little lie.

"Somebody's going to have to go get your mama and papa," she said.

"We don't have a mama; she died," Nola whispered, staring at her plate.

"I see I'm not gonna get anything out of you two; I'll just wait till Glen and them boys get back and see what to do," Alma said. "Did you say something, little girl?" she said looking at Nola.

"Eat your food, Nola," I interrupted, seeing she hadn't touched a bite.

"Not hungry," she muttered.

"I'll take what you don't want," said James.

"Go ahead," I told him. "She won't eat it."

"Ma, is it okay?" James said, before rising.

"Fine by me. But Miss, you're gonna get hungry later."

"Go ahead," Nola said and handed him her plate.

As we were eating, the cats started patrolling. They smelled food and were cagey enough to rush by Alma before she could see them.

Alma got up several times and said, "Scat!" and stomped her foot.

"How's your sting?" she asked.

I looked down at my arm slathered with snuff. It didn't look too nice, but the snuff was a cure.

"Fine," I said and hoped I could find some water to wash that stuff off while Alma wasn't looking.

Before we left the kitchen, Alma got out the Bible and began reading silently. She laid it down on the table, closed her eyes, and bowed her head.

"Lord, help us to convert these children to know the truth of your ways."

"We know the truth!" Nola squealed. "We have our own church."

"Not the right church," Alma said quietly.

"I want my daddy! I want my brothers!" Nola said. "We can't stay here, Ella. What if she baptizes us and makes us join Saints of Calvary?"

"Come on, Nola. You're tired," I said. "Let me take you out for a little walk in the yard. That all right with you, Alma?"

"Yes," Alma said sternly, "she needs to get calmed down."

Meanwhile none of the other children said a word. Well behaved didn't come close to describing this family. It was as if they were trapped in prison.

I took Nola's hand, and we walked slowly around the yard, dodging cats.

"Nola, if the boys aren't here by sundown, we're going to find them," I said. "This family gives me the creeps."

"If Saints of Calvary are the ones who know the truth, why does Alma dip snuff? It's nasty!" she said.

"I think it's her medicine," I said. "I heard her threaten her kids when she doctored me. She told them they better not tell their pa about her snuff, that she was using it for medicinal purposes."

About that time I heard a train whistle, and so I figured we weren't so far away from Little Rock that Daddy couldn't find us. I hoped Daddy was already looking for us. We had gone from the frying pan into the fire on this little journey.

All the men came in after dark tired and hungry. Dewey bounced in and said he was starving for a drink.

"Don't touch those glasses!" Nola hissed. "The dad-burned cats have licked all over them."

Alma turned around and looked at Nola.

"Miss, we don't swear in this house," she said gruffly.

After Alma and Glen kicked cats out of the way and said scat several times, supper was served. Once again, it was pinto beans, fried potatoes, and cornbread, and plenty of it. I didn't care if the cats had licked off the plates with their bare tongues. We were starving, and Alma was a good cook.

"Ja get that wagon fixed?" Alma asked Glen.

"Yes'm, it's fixed. Next, we have to find some beds for these young fellers. They're orphans, you know."

McKinley gave me the look, and I pinched Nola to stay quiet. Why did the boys have to say we were orphans?

While the men and boys went outside to talk about machinery and farm animals and other dull stuff, all the women and girls had to wash and dry dishes. When we were through, Alma cleaned more beans to soak overnight for tomorrow's dinner. She surely liked beans.

"Are we sleeping here?" Nola asked.

"You sure are, Miss," said Alma and laughed heartily. "Gonna make up some Methodist pallets in the house, and the boys can sleep on the porch," she continued and laughed.

Dewey stomped through the house looking for another drink of water. He spied Esther, who was pretty as a picture and quiet as a mouse.

"What's the matter? Cat got your tongue?" He laughed.

"No sir," she said.

"How old are you?" asked Dew.

"She's eleven, Mister," Alma said. "Now, you go on out there with the men."

He started out and then turned to me.

"Sister, I need to talk to you about something. Come outside in a little while," he said quietly.

When I went out to talk to him, he told me McKinley wanted to escape during the night.

"I'm there," I said. "I liked cats until now, but they're overloaded here."

"Not only that," Dew said, "but Mr. Porter tried to convert us and make us Saints of Calvary. He said we're in the last days."

"What if he's right, Dew?" I asked.

"I can't help it if it is. When Glen told me we were going to have to burn our instruments, that was the last straw for me. He said they're works of the devil."

"What did you say to him?"

"I just told him the devil sure knows how to invent something that plays pretty music. But that didn't set too well with him."

"Oh, Dew! We better get out of here!"

"That's the plan. We'll wait until everybody's asleep, and I'll go hook up the wagon. McKinley will get you and Nola and bring you to the barn."

So it was that after the Bible reading and a long prayer, we lay down on our Methodist pallets. Nola and I stayed awake, waiting nervously for McKinley. Finally, when Alma and Glen were snoring loud as machine guns, McKinley crept in the back door and touched me on the shoulder.

We tiptoed out the back door so the Porter boys sleeping on the porch wouldn't see us. The only light in the sky came from the moon periodically peeking out from the clouds.

Dew and McKinley walked the team down to the main road, and we all got in the wagon as cats scampered everywhere.

"Dew, can you drive?" asked McKinley. "I'm beat."

"Sure, bud," he said.

The clouds were swimming lazily in the sky, and we couldn't see any direction. Dewey drove the team slowly to stay out of the ditches.

"Boy, that was a close call," he said to me. "That Mr. Porter really wanted us to be his orphans and become Saints of Calvary."

"I think his wife wanted the same," I said. "Let's get to Pine Bluff as fast as we can!"

Dewey drove nearly all night while McKinley slept. Nola and I slept between bumping up and down rough spots on the road. As dawn broke, Dewey started yelling excitedly.

"Bud, wake up! I see lights!" he said.

Oh, blissful rest. We could go to Aunt Leah's, and she'd fix us breakfast and let us sleep some more.

I sat up and squinted, trying to wake up. Something wasn't right.

McKinley raised up when the mules began to act funny. They balked, and when Dewey tried to make them go, they reared up.

"Jump out!" McKinley said. We're on top of the tracks, and a train's coming!"

CHAPTER 35

AFTER THE ACCIDENT

That's when the train's whistle sounded loud and clear. I felt the tracks vibrating; we were right smack on top of them. Dewey shoved Nola and me, and we fell to the earth with a sickening thud. It knocked the breath out of me. I tried to breathe in oxygen, but my lungs felt frozen to my chest.

I called out, but as in a bad dream, no words would come. I saw the sun coming up, and the world went black just as Mama told me to be still.

"Ella!" said the voice, but when I opened my eyes, it was Nola standing over me crying and saying my name. "The wagon fell on top of you!"

Two men were lifting the wagon up while another man pulled me out. I inhaled a shallow and painful breath and lay back on the cool dirt of the embankment. Then there was darkness all around me, and I could hear voices way in the distance.

I opened my eyes, and Lethie was sitting beside me. Why was she in Pine Bluff? This looked like our room in Little Rock, but I couldn't get the words out to ask. My eyes asked questions, and Lethie jumped up and ran out into the hall.

"Ella's awake! Praise the Lord, she comin' to," she said to someone.

Daddy walked in and kneeled beside my bed.

"You're back with us, Sister. How do you feel?"

I tried to make him understand how confused I was with my eyes.

"You were in an accident, Sister. You were trying to get to Pine Bluff, but Dewey left that Porter house and went the wrong direction, and you ended back here on the railroad tracks in Little Rock."

His last words trailed off into the quiet, and I lost consciousness again.

I was in and out of sleep a long time, but I heard activity going on all around me. Where was Nola? Where were the boys? What happened to the mules? Did we cause the train to wreck? How did Daddy find us? No one could tell me because I couldn't ask.

Finally, one day I woke up to find Nola looking down at me.

"Are you awake, Sister?"

"Yes," said my voice, but I didn't recognize it.

"Want me to get you some coffee milk?" she asked.

I didn't have to answer in words. Before long I had coffee milk and Daddy, Nola, and the boys in my room.

"How long has it been?" I asked, unable to move without a sharp knifelike pain in my chest.

"Just a few days," Daddy said. "The doctor has been seeing to you, and you're going to be fine. You just had an injury to your chest."

"Where's Lethie?"

"Right here, honey," she said, coming over to me from a dark corner of the room.

Then the story of those few days missing from my memory came to life.

Dewey had turned the wagon right instead of left leaving the Porters. He drove through the night without much light except for the moon, which stayed behind the clouds much of the time. We arrived back at the outskirts of Little Rock, not knowing we were passing over the train tracks. The mules' instincts were heightened when they felt the vibrations of the train coming, and their fear caused them to react. If they had not, none of us would be alive to tell about it.

The train was able to brake, and the men working on it got out and rescued us. Nola was scratched up, and McKinley and Dewey were thrown into the gully below. The only one harmed was me.

Daddy was already on his way home when the accident happened. Lethie had been worried sick when we hadn't come in from school. She had taken the letter McKinley had written and asked a neighbor to read it to her. It told the whole story of why we were leaving Little Rock.

"Are we in bad trouble?" I asked in a small voice I didn't recognize.

"Yeah, go out and get me a switch for your whipping," Daddy said and laughed. Then he got very quiet and squeezed my hand.

"All that matters now is getting you well," he said.

But I knew my getting well wasn't the only thing that was important. Daddy had to work on fixing the problems in our family. If he was going to stay married to Miss Rhodie, we would all have to adjust.

As I healed, I tried to adapt. Miss Rhodie came home from Oklahoma and worked at being pleasant. Maybe Daddy had had a talk with her, but she chatted with each of us individually and said she wanted us to be a family. In the meantime other crises were going on in the family and in the world.

In January of 1918 McKinley finished school. He was intent on joining the army and going to France to fight.

One morning I woke up before daylight and heard the boys talking. I put on my robe and walked downstairs, where they were huddled in front of the fireplace. They stopped when I appeared.

"What's the secret talk about?" I asked.

"Oh, it's war talk, Ella," McKinley said as he took a quick drink of coffee. Dewey walked over to the fire and threw a newspaper in.

"Bud, quit that!" McKinley yelled. "You'll set the house on fire!" But Dewey couldn't stop, because he was Dewey, all energy and fire himself.

"What about the war?" I asked McKinley, curious as to why he looked so serious.

"I'm joining up," he said. "Already talked to Daddy about it."

"Where will you go?" I asked.

"Over to Camp Pike, not too far from here."

"Then will you go to Europe?" I asked.

"Most likely," he said.

"Explain to me who's fighting who, McKinley."

"Okay. The US has allies—France, Britain, and Russia—and we've agreed to help them fight Germany, Austria, and Hungary."

"Show me a map," Dewey said. "I want to see where the fighting is going on."

"Daddy has an old one rolled up in the trunk. Get it out and we'll take a look at it."

McKinley looked so grown-up talking like this. He was beginning to need to shave his face often, and his arms looked like a grown man's now. I sat down beside him and waited for the map.

"McKinley, why is everyone so mad at each other that they're willing to kill?" I asked.

"It boils down to the fact that everybody wants to operate in their own way. Sometimes, the people at the top want more power. Countries fight over land. War is nasty business," McKinley said.

Dewey brought in the map, and McKinley pointed out the countries he had told us about. Dewey asked McKinley if he was scared.

"No siree, I'm not scared. I'm proud to fight. As I see it, what was not right was the Germans sinking the *Lusitania* in '15. I read that spark started the whole war."

"Don't be telling Miss Rhodie you're fighting the Germans. Her people are from Germany," said Dewey.

"Oh, you can bet on that," said McKinley. "I can just hear her now starting to rant and rave about the war."

To tell the truth, I didn't understand why people would kill each other to get their own way. There was plenty of land in the world, enough for everybody. However, McKinley was sure of himself, and McKinley acted as if he knew the truth about everything. Somehow, I knew he would be safe across the Atlantic Ocean fighting with the doughboys.

"Will you write to us?" I asked.

"If I have time, Sister," he said and stared at the fireplace like Daddy did.

"We'll write you, McKinley," I said and hugged him, which he would rarely let me do.

Soon after that, Daddy took McKinley over to Fort Pike for his enlistment.

When Daddy got home, I asked him how McKinley took to the army.

"He was ready, Ella. After McKinley gets trained, his outfit will probably be shipped to the western front."

We started writing letters back and forth every few days, even though Fort Pike wasn't that far from us. McKinley had to stay put through boot camp without any interference.

Dewey eagerly went to the post office every day, hoping for a letter.

"Ella, we got a letter from McKinley today," Dewey said the first time Daddy had gone off to work.

"Read it to us."

"Do you think it's okay to open it without Daddy here?"

"We're the bosses while Daddy's gone, so yes!" I said.

He tore into the letter and began reading:

Dear Family,

I'm now officially a foot soldier in the 173rd Airborne. Long before you get up, I'm out of my bunk, getting ready for the day in a hurry. When the bugle blows, we have to be up and ready to go in short order. I have been doing drills and target practice. I think I'll make marksman before long. The weather here has been cold, so that makes the marching pretty hard on some days. I'm told we'll probably be deployed to France when we've finished training. Daddy, please mail me some of my books, as there's nothing to read here. Tell Dewey and the girls hello and to write when they can. Tell Lethie I sure do miss her cooking—the mess hall doesn't match it.

Your loving son,

McKinley

Dewey sat staring into space.

"Wish I could go fight the Krauts," he said.

"Don't be goofy, Dewey," I said. "You're too young."

"Hush up, Sister."

And so it went until Nola put her hands over her ears to deafen the noise.

When we went to bed, Nola said she had a deep-purple headache and felt queasy. I touched her forehead, and she was hot with fever.

I gave her an aspirin and put a cool washcloth on her head. I decided to make up with Dewey and ask him to check on Nola.

"Don't you be getting that old Spanish flu," Dewey said. "It's just about getting to everybody these days."

"Daddy told me about the Spanish flu. I wonder if Nola started it or if the sickness she had just left her more likely to get it," I said.

"I imagine her kind of flu was some other kind. McKinley said our soldiers got the Spanish flu here and took it to Europe with them. It caused lots of people to die on both continents," he said.

"I hope she's better by morning," I said. "I can't take her being sick again," I said, thinking of myself as much as her.

"Maybe her body built up enough strength from the last flu that she won't have a bad case of it," said Dewey the physician.

"If this time is as bad as the last, I don't think she can survive," I said pessimistically.

CHAPTER 36

OFF TO WAR

Nola had a bad cold; that's all it was, thankfully, and we went on about our lives as usual, except for one thing. McKinley had been sent to France.

The war was being fought in trenches, which the doughboys had to dig out themselves. The enemy had to do the same. There was a piece of land across the horizon separating France and us called No Man's Land. This stretched about four hundred miles across Western Europe. Each side had big cannons.

"I wish I could fight with McKinley," Dewey said to Daddy, who had just come in from the railroad.

"McKinley will take care of it for you," Daddy said. "Children, this is nothing for you to worry about. God has prepared McKinley for this moment, and he is ready."

"Will McKinley get hurt?" Nola said, biting her nails. Since she had stopped sucking her thumb, she'd taken up nail-biting.

"We pray that he doesn't," Daddy said. "Life works the way it should, and McKinley will be fine."

Daddy believed in always telling us what was going on. He thought we could handle it. But I just didn't understand war at all.

"Let's go in and visit with Miss Rhodie, children. Daddy has to leave tomorrow," he said in third person.

"Am I in charge of these two when you go?" Dewey asked.

"That you are," Daddy said. "By the way, Son, I want to tell you something about the car. If you ever have an emergency, you have my permission to drive it."

"Only in an emergency?" Dewey asked.

"Yes!" Daddy said. "Emergency means someone's life is at stake. Anything short of that is not an emergency."

After we sat with Miss Rhodie a few minutes, just enough to be polite, Daddy said he and Dewey needed to check the car. Then they went out and placed the tarp over Her Majesty so the weather wouldn't get to her.

Daddy didn't bring out the guitar that night. He said he just wanted to sit on the porch and hear our voices. He told Dewey to be responsible for checking our lessons, and I told him I would help Nola with hers.

Lethie stuck her head out the door. "Just saying good-night, you'ens. Have a good rest, and blow out the lamps on the way in."

I shivered going into the house, but not so much from the chilly evening. I was thinking about McKinley sitting in a wet fox-hole with rats and bugs and gunfire. I wondered if he'd caught Spanish influenza and was lying sick with fever. I wondered if he could shoot a man.

In the days ahead, Nola and I occupied ourselves by teaching Lethie to read. At first she was scared, but we showed her just how easy it was.

"Pretty soon, you babies'll have me writin' too." She laughed and slapped her hip.

Daddy and Miss Rhodie tried to stay civil, but it didn't take long for the bickering to start again. I learned to cope by escaping into a book. Nola was attached to Lethie and spent a lot more time with her. Dewey was just Dewey and didn't attempt to keep things on an even keel. He had his mind on becoming a doctor so much that he had trouble focusing on reading and spelling. I wasn't much in the arithmetic department, but I made the spelling bees.

Daddy had Nola and me take Expression and singing lessons from two ladies in town. They came to school every Thursday and taught anyone interested. Misses Bertie and Gertie Shaw were known in Little Rock as the old-maid twins. Both taught us popular songs of the day as well as ballads. They were fairly old, at least forty, and dabbed perfume all over themselves, even their clothes. They still lived with their mama and papa and one grandpa.

"Nola doesn't like singing," said Miss Bertie to me one day.

"Miss Bertie," I said, "I don't mean anything against my little sister, but she even scares the chickens away when she tries to carry a tune."

Miss Bertie laughed hard and said that maybe Nola needed to take something other than singing lessons.

"But you, my dear can sing well. I love to hear your voice and I might start teaching you more diverse music if you'd like." That was all right by me.

The twins always wore hats with hatpins stuck in them and hobble skirts from 1910. These dresses were fitted right below the knee and flared out, causing Bertie and Gertie a lot of frustration because they had to take such tiny steps to walk. They were always mentioning their corsets too, saying they couldn't wait to get home and peel the tight things off.

"Nola," I said one day, "you might as well start looking for a husband, because you're not trying to do anything with your life."

"That's just what I want: a handsome husband who has lots of money and a big car. I'll have diamond sparkles all over my fingers, and most of all I want lots of babies."

"It'll be more fun being a singer," I bragged. "Miss Bertie and Miss Gertie said I have a nice voice."

"Pride goeth before the fall, Sister," she said. "Miss Rhodie won't ever let you be a singer."

"Just wait," I said. "Someday I'm going out to Hollywood and make a million dollars a year in the movies like Mae West. Then, I'm coming after Daddy and taking him to California with me, and we'll have lemon and orange trees. If you're nice, I'll let you come too."

"Oh, I'll be nice, because I'll be living in my mansion with a maid and butler."

"Pride goeth before the fall, Nola," I said, and practiced my elocution with mouth wide open as the sisters had instructed me.

Dreaming is one thing God expects everyone to do. But my dreaming wasn't within the bounds of what He was offering.

I remember well when God put me in my place and showed me I was too big for my britches, because it was on that day that my hair started falling out by the handfuls.

My thick dark hair had been one thing I didn't mind about myself. It had been a few years since it had been cut, and it fell way down my back. I began to notice every time I washed it, a big glob would come out in the comb. At first I thought it was a coincidence. But every day it got worse, and I finally went to Lethie with my problem.

"Honey," she said, "you gots to show Miss Rhodie. You gon' lose all yo' hair if you don't do sumpin."

I protested and made her promise not to tell. I tried to hide the spots by braiding my hair and putting it on top of my head. I always found an excuse to wear a scarf when we went somewhere.

When Daddy came home, he used his instincts to identify the problem.

"Sister, we have to find a doctor. It's pathetic that Rhodie and I have made such a mess of our lives that the strain has gotten to you."

"Oh, Daddy, I'm not letting anything worry me," I said. "Maybe it's the soap I'm using."

"Rhodie," he said turning to her, "we've got to find Ella a doctor. This is not right."

"She's washing her hair too often," Miss Rhodie said, but she went to get a coat to go with us.

The doctor began to look at my scalp. He took a brush, stroked my hair gently, and looked at the brush again. He examined the bare spots on my head again.

"Alopecia areata," he said.

"Huh?" I asked.

"Baldness in spots. Have you ever been really sick with a high fever, Miss?" he asked.

"No sir," I said.

"Can you think of anything that might have caused damage to your scalp?"

"The children had lice infestation," Miss Rhodie chimed in.

"That may be your answer," he said. "We'll treat the scalp so it doesn't cause any more damage."

I began to cry. "Will it all fall out?"

"I don't think so, Miss. Just take care of what you have left."

When we got back to the farm, Miss Rhodie was very quiet. Daddy turned to her.

"Rhodie, you should have been treating this weeks ago," he said. "Ella's losing a lot of her hair, and you could have saved it from happening."

"Pardon me, but I didn't know the girl's hair was falling out."

"Now you do. I expect you to help my children even if you and I don't agree on things."

I sat in my window that night looking out at the stars. The smell of rain drifted in, and I knew it was coming soon. I had always liked that smell. I just wished I could feel better about my hair. It wasn't fair for a girl to have trouble with her only decent feature.

As I pitied my condition, Nola came in and started looking for her gown. She left things in such a mess, it was hard to find my own things, being perfect and all.

"What's wrong, Sister? Are you crying?"

"Not really. Just thinking about my hair."

"I have some news that'll make you feel better. I heard Daddy talking to Rhodie, and we are divorcing her and moving back to Pine Bluff."

"Well, Nola, that's kinda sad. Poor Lethie! What'll she do without us?"

"I know," she said. "But think what this means for us. We'll be home again."

My heart fluttered. We would be with our family again, and Kit and I could be best friends and confide in each other like we used to.

"And listen to what Rhodie said to Daddy. She told him to just go, and she would give him part of her place to sell for cash. She said now that women can sign contracts in Arkansas and own property openly, she can do this. Said it would be worth it to her to get Daddy out of here."

"What did Daddy say?" I asked.

"He said, 'No, thank you, Rhodie. I don't want your land. I've always felt beholden to you for moving my family in. But I've supported you with my money throughout these years, and I don't feel like I got anything in return. No life at all would be better than this.'"

"Good for Daddy," I said. "It was Rhodie who wanted us to move here instead of her moving to Pine Bluff, so the land is not Daddy's problem."

"Do you know how nice it'll be with just us and not the two of them insulting each other all the time?" Nola said.

"Oh, yes," I said and fell over on the bed, starting to cry.

"Sister, I don't understand you sometimes," Nola said.

"I don't understand me either. I just cry for nothing anymore."

Someone knocked on our door softly, opened it, and came over to the bed.

"What's wrong, honeys?" Lethie asked. "Who's crying in here?"

"It's Sister," Nola said. "She's crying again."

Lethie sat down beside me and began to run her fingers through my hair. It felt so good that I closed my eyes.

"What's wrong with me?" I asked her. "All I do is cry and get my feelings hurt."

"Ella, you about to start you period," she said. "Them little materials in your body rolling around getting all mixed up with each other, and they saying 'get me straight, get me straight!'"

She went on to explain nature and the way girls turn into women, and I felt self-conscious from my head to my toes.

"You don't understand…" I began.

"Oh, but I do," Lethie said, wiping off her face with the tail of her apron. "I been a woman a long time. I used to be a girl too. I know what the young years do to you, and I know you gonna be mad half the time. You gonna think nobody act right but you. You gonna think nobody wear the right togs but you. You gonna be ashamed of yo' daddy and Miss Rhodie 'cause they don't know nothing no more. You gonna want to act like you don't know none of us. But we here for you, Ella, when you come back down to earth."

"All I want is to stay out of people's business and vice versa," I said.

"Honey, you ain't got no business but to grow up into a woman. Them five or six years is rocky between now and when you get your senses back. Just let the Lord help you from one stone to the next, and you'll get over Fool's Hill."

I didn't want to hear preaching, and I didn't like it that Lethie wiped her face on her apron she cooked in. I thought to myself she didn't know about anything in real life.

She went off muttering to herself, "Versa vicea, vice versa, what does Lethie know?"

Adding to my other worries, including Lethie's accusation that I was stuck on my own self, was another reality.

Our nation was at war, and my brother was right in the middle of it as we would later learn. We sat close to our Sears and Roebuck 1909 Silverton radio in those days listening together as a family for news that the conflict was ending. Though Miss Rhodie had enough compassion to worry about McKinley, her loyalty was divided because of concern for her people in Germany.

Sometimes she got down right obstinate. Though the president urged American citizens to supply their own needs, she balked at planting a garden. Instead, Daddy, Dewey, Nola and I planted green beans, squash, potatoes, and other delicious vegetables to honor the cause. There was no actual food rationing during the war, but people were urged to have "Meatless Meals," "Wheatless Wednesdays," and to remember that "Food Will Win the War."

Miss Rhodie refused to buy enough flour and sugar to supply poor Lethie items she needed for baking, making pancakes and other goodies. It made one wonder if Miss Rhodie did really want victory over the Germans.

She and Daddy simply stayed away from each other as much as possible now. She didn't talk with us kids anymore either. Dew and I spent the entire month of June waiting for the other shoe to drop, but the two of them kept a peaceful silence.

On June 28, the war ended, and McKinley sent Daddy a telegram saying he would be home soon.

When Miss Rhodie read the telegram, she told Daddy she wanted to go visit her cousin in Tulsa soon and take Lethie with her.

I thought her timing was strange. But little mice with big ears lived in our house, and Dewey heard what she told Daddy.

"Your people call those of us who are born of the Germanic persuasion such terrible, filthy names. I can't abide hearing those victory war stories when McKinley gets back here. I've got to get away!"

Daddy and Rhodie talked even less to each other after that. The next several days, we all walked on eggshells. The veil of gloom could be cut with a butter knife. Eventually, Miss Rhodie persuaded Lethie to go along with her to Tulsa.

I stopped concentrating on the strain of our household and waited impatiently for McKinley to come home. He arrived in Boston on the USS *George Washington* in August. He took the train to Arkansas, and it was an exciting day when we met him at the station in Little Rock.

When he came down the steps, he looked so grown-up in his pressed khaki uniform and army hat. We all grabbed him and hugged him. Then, Daddy squashed us all in the car, and McKinley took off his hat. His head was shaved, and he didn't look like himself at all up close. Later we would squeeze little facts out of him, one by one, about the shaved head and about the front in France. But right that moment, he wasn't talking. He had a terrible hoarse cough.

All the way home, Dewey asked McKinley questions about the war. He asked what kind of medicine they gave people who were injured and how they were bandaged up. McKinley had always been long on words, but now he was so quiet I wondered what was going through his head. He mainly stared out the window like his mind was a million miles away. He kept coughing his head off. It wasn't a cough like Nola had with the flu, although hers was bad. It was different.

When we finally got to bed that night, McKinley fell asleep as soon as his head hit the pillow. Before my eyes closed, I heard him moaning in the darkness. Daddy went in and shook him awake.

"Son, you had a bad dream. Want to talk about it?"

"It was the mustard gas that got him," McKinley said.

"Who?" Daddy asked.

"A buddy of mine."

McKinley got up and put on his clothes, and he and Daddy went to the porch. I listened quietly. I couldn't figure out why McKinley wasn't happier to be home.

"The Krauts attacked us with poison gas. Everything was exploding around us, and we were stuck in our foxholes days on end, dealing with bugs and rats. All that kept our brains together was friendship. But I lost a good friend when they gassed us. His gas mask didn't work."

"How did our boys do in the fighting end of things?" Daddy asked.

"Our company didn't see much action because the war was coming to a close. The boys before us are the ones who made a difference," McKinley said.

"We think life is precious, but in war life is cheap, isn't it, Son?" Daddy said.

"Yeah," McKinley said. "I can't get the smell of disinfecting lime and the stench of corpses out of my nostrils. I can't get the sound of artillery shells out of my ears. Daddy, I'm pretty messed up right now." He coughed some more.

The next morning he was asleep when I got up. Daddy was worn out and said they had talked nearly all night.

"Why is his head shaved?" Nola asked.

"When the boys got home, they got deloused. McKinley was eaten up with lice. He's just lucky he came home in one piece."

"He's got a bad cough too," I said.

"It was always damp in those foxholes," Daddy said. "If the gas didn't blind or suffocate those boys, the damp got them. It's sickening what man does to his fellow man."

"We'll get McKinley well," Dr. Dewey said. "I've read up on the war, and some guys lose their minds just thinking about what happened."

"We won't let McKinley do that," Daddy said.

But McKinley started moaning again. I went in to check on him, and he had his face covered with his hands. He was shaking.

"McKinley, wake up! You're home and we're here for you," I said.

He sat up, looking confused, and didn't answer me. He got out of bed and went to the rocker on the porch. Daddy brought him some coffee, and he sat there all day, staring across the yard and not talking.

McKinley's cough would improve for a while and then get bad again. Finally, the local doctor told Daddy he was going to write the army. McKinley had been gassed in France, and it had damaged his lungs. The doctor would ask for a medical discharge for McKinley.

"I want an honorable discharge," McKinley said with unfeeling eyes. "Don't get any medical discharge for me."

"Medical is honorable, McKinley," Daddy said. "This is no blight on your army record. You've got damaged lungs."

"I have some finishing up to do, Daddy. I have to—for all the guys who didn't make it back home."

"They'd want you right here getting well where you belong," Daddy said.

Reluctantly, McKinley agreed to let the doctor contact the army, and he was medically discharged. Even I could see he had a long way to go to get well, both with his lungs and his way of thinking.

Soon after that, Daddy announced we were moving back to Pine Bluff. The land he'd wanted years ago was available, and he was ready to get back home. He was by no means alone with that thought; everyone in the household was ready.

It just so happened that two days before we left, Miss Rhodie and Lethie returned to the house. Miss Rhodie was still unhappy, and Lethie was on the verge of tears.

When Nola and I began packing our belongings, Miss Rhodie came into our room. She looked like she hadn't slept and sat down on my bed, just watching us empty our closets.

I couldn't think of anything to say, so I continued pulling stockings and undergarments out of my drawer and dumping them into my trunk.

"I won't be going with you to Pine Bluff," Rhodie said. "Your daddy seems to think we need some time apart."

"Yes ma'am, I know," I said quietly.

Nola kept on with the motions of packing, not saying a word. I knew if she turned around, she would say something hateful to Miss Rhodie, and it wasn't the time.

"You take care of Lethie, will you?" I said.

Rhodie jumped up abruptly and went to the door, her body stiff.

"I say I'm not going with your father to his new home and all you can say is 'take care of Lethie'? Haven't I been the one instrumental in seeing to your schooling? Haven't I taught you proper etiquette? And who hid the fact that your daddy has turned into a drunkard from you? Not Lethie. Oh, no, not her. It was I who pulled all the load around here, and this is the thanks I get!"

No doubt Miss Rhodie was ready to get us out of her sight. We heard her shoes clop heavily all the way down the stairs. All I heard out of the whole tirade was that Daddy was a drunkard, and I doubted that. Anyway, I would ask him someday when we were far away in Pine Bluff, and Miss Rhodie would be in Little Rock still pulling the entire load.

We started out before early light one morning in late summer. Rhodie didn't make an appearance. Lethie stood at the door and handed us food for the trip, as though this was only a temporary thing.

"You uns be safe now," she said, but her toothy grin was false, and her eyes glistened.

"Keep up your reading, Lethie," was all Nola said, but she turned and hugged her tightly.

I put my heart and mind in another place so I wouldn't cry. Lethie had been with us through some mighty storms.

"Bye, Lethie!" I said as I slipped into Her Majesty.

"Bye, honeys," she said and closed the door before Daddy started the car.

Dewey drove the wagon, and McKinley pulled out the lazy board to sit on. They carried our accumulation of household items from our time in Little Rock. Daddy and we girls pulled a trailer with the car.

Daddy took off slowly and looked back at the place sadly.

"Got to take it pretty slow today," he said. "Pulling the trailer is hard on the car."

It felt funny leaving that big house with so many memories still in it. Even with Daddy and Rhodie's problems, we were just children, and looked at life as though it was filled with sunshine. I would miss Lethie and some friends I had made. But I could hardly wait to see Kit and Aunt Leah. Maybe Daddy would even let us go get little Daniel.

"Are you a drunkard, Daddy?" Nola asked as we drove along the road. I expected him to give her the look and ignore the question. Instead he gave us a surprising answer.

"I have been drinking some, girls. It's just to self-medicate myself from the miseries of Little Rock. I never should have married that woman! I can promise you now and forever, though, that I will never have another drink of anything."

I didn't want to dispute his word about the miseries of Little Rock, and I didn't want it to be true that he had been drinking liquor. But I had to believe his promise that he wouldn't drink again.

I sat looking out the window as the day passed by. We stopped off in a nearby community and spent the night in a boardinghouse, as our car didn't have headlights. The next morning we ate a hearty breakfast with the local regulars at the house and made it to Pine Bluff by afternoon.

My stomach began to flutter at the thought of seeing my own people again.

"Can we go to Aunt Leah's first?" I asked.

"Yes, we'll stop there. Aunt Leah has invited us to stay at her house until we get our land and house in order," Daddy said.

Nola and I both were out the door before Daddy officially stopped the car. Kit ran out to meet us.

"Are you Kit?" Nola said. She didn't look like our cousin at all.

"What do you mean, is this me?" Kit shouted. She hugged us both so tightly I thought we would burst. We kissed each other's cheeks, and I stood way back and looked at her.

She was almost fifteen now and half a head taller than I was. She had her dark-brown hair in the latest style with puffs over the ears. Her face wasn't just cute anymore; it was pretty. She had curves and a different way about her. Kit had grown up!

"What happened to your eyes?" Kit asked me.

"I've been crying the whole trip. Why can't I stop, Kit? I'm happy as can be about moving back," I said.

"I do the same thing, Ella. It's like I cry even when I'm happy," she said. She stood with Nola and me on each side of her, and we all linked arms. She towered over both of us, and I felt very envious.

Little Becca came out of the house, and I could hardly believe my eyes. She was a good-sized little girl now. She still had her blond hair, all curled in ringlets. I wished she could know my little brother, only months older than she was.

I wondered what Lethie was doing right now. I bet she was washing dishes and singing with that toothy grin of hers. It seemed that someone was always going away from us or versa vicea, as Lethie would say.

I slipped out of my sorrow when Aunt Leah served supper. She had new potatoes, green beans, pork chops, biscuits, and gravy. We left not a morsel on our plates.

She asked us girls to do the dishes, so Kit and Becca washed while Nola and I dried.

"Do you remember that boy we used to think was so cute named Troy Clark?" Kit said.

"Sure," I said. "He and McKinley keep in touch because of their music."

"Does he still live here?" Nola asked.

"He went to Little Rock for a while, but now he's back," she said. "He's taken me a place or two, but Mama says he is too old for me to go with."

I remembered the times I had thought about Troy and how I was going to marry him someday. I guessed Kit had forgotten about that and gone with him anyway.

"Girls, hurry," Uncle Josh said. "Leah and the guys are about to start the music."

We rushed through wiping the dishes, stacking them where we could find a spot. We didn't want to miss any part of the action. Uncle Josh was talking to Daddy when we went to the parlor.

"Jim," Uncle Josh said, "Some guy with a young boy came by here looking for you the other day. Didn't get his name though."

"Don't know who that would be. What'd he look like?"

"He had lost a leg and was pretty frail," Uncle Josh said. "Was on crutches."

"Pop, they came by here the other day while everybody was gone too," Kit said.

"Everybody wasn't gone. You and me were here," said Becca, hanging on to Kit's arm.

"Becca, go on and don't bother us now. We're visiting," she said and shooed her away.

Kit turned to me. "Drives me crazy," she said. "She wants to be right here on me every minute."

"See, if you'd had a little brother, you wouldn't have to worry about it," I said.

"Ha ha! Now that would be worse!" she said and hugged me again.

Aunt Leah pulled out the piano stool.

"Jim, you ready to make some music?" she asked Daddy, sitting down at the piano.

"Let's do it," Daddy said, picking up his guitar. Aunt Leah fell right in with the beat, just like old times. Life felt good—no, better than good. I sang my heart out with Kit and Aunt Leah to "Put on Your Old Gray Bonnet," "Old Kentucky Home," "Swing Low, Sweet Chariot," and "I Wonder Who's Kissing Her Now." Finally, I closed my eyes and lay back, hoping this was not a dream.

"Are you daydreaming again, Sister?" Daddy asked as he picked up his guitar and began strumming. I didn't answer.

"Sleep, baby, sleep, close your bright eyes, listen to your Daddy as he sings a lullaby," Daddy sang softly, then stopped abruptly.

"Off to bed, you two," he said to Nola and me, laying down his guitar. "Tomorrow's a big day."

We went into Kit's room and got ready for bed. It was the same as when we were little. Kit and Nola put me in the middle of her double bed, and it was a tight fit, given that we had bigger bodies now.

"I've got a secret," Kit whispered as she pulled something from the back of her nightstand.

"What? What?" I said.

She put a ring on her finger and held up her hand to show us.

"I'm getting married," Kit said, "and this is my engagement ring."

It was a small gold band with a tiny diamond in the middle.

"Kit, I can't believe it! Are your folks all right with this?"

"Shhhh. We're eloping. Daddy and Mama won't sign for us."

"Why do you want to get married right now? You're not old enough, Kit," Nola said.

"I love him. You'll love him too...but I can't say his name because I promised not to say a word."

"I hope you know what you're doing," I said, disappointed. "I was hoping we could be best friends again."

"Being married won't change that, Ella," Kit said.

"Just don't move from here. That's all I ask."

Nola and I were so shocked and so tired, we said nothing more. Then Kit snuffed out the lamp and tried to cheer us up by asking us about our adventures in Little Rock. That opened up the dam of memories.

Nola told the story about our stay at the Porters' farm. The more we recalled, the funnier it got, and we were giggling so hard Nola fell off the bed.

"Pipe down in there, girls," Daddy said from the parlor.

"Yessir, Daddy," I said and went into spasms of laughter again.

"Remember that snuff Alma put on your bee sting?" Nola sputtered through raspy hysteria.

"And the eighteen cats we had to fight off us?" I said, buckling in fits of laughter.

But Daddy rained on our parade and burst through the door fuming.

"Go to sleep," he said with his mouth pressed tightly.

"Sorry, Daddy, we're just excited," Nola said.

"Go to sleep," he said again sternly.

We tried. We really did. But the big four poster that held so many memories of three little girls had been outgrown. I tried to lie still, but the girls were suffocating me. Finally, I shut my eyes, and the next thing I knew, Becca was yelling for us to get up. Aunt Leah's bacon was frying, and Daddy was already tuning his guitar.

That morning none of us knew that within a few weeks, life would take an unexpected turn.

CHAPTER 37

BIG CHANGES AHEAD

It was the week before Armistice Day when I first caught a glimpse of the man and the boy. McKinley and I were shopping for house paint at the hardware store when they walked by, the man swinging along on crutches and a young auburn-haired boy holding on to his arm. They stopped, the boy looked up at the man and said something to him, and both looked through the window at me.

"Who is that looking in here?" I asked the clerk.

"Don't know. Never saw them before."

Since they were looking at me like they knew me, I ran out of the store to speak to them. By that time they had gotten into their wagon and were about to leave.

"Hey!" I said. "Are you looking for somebody?"

The boy turned around and stared at me. He shook his head no, and they rode off in the mist of the morning.

I thought no more about it. McKinley put the paint and brushes in Her Majesty, and we left for home.

Daddy had bought twenty acres not far from Aunt Leah's and Uncle Josh's farm.

The old farmhouse was begging for attention, and Daddy decided the boys should paint the house.

We had a few days left with Daddy, and he wanted to get the place livable in the meantime.

When we drove up, Uncle Josh's wagon was parked in front of the house. As we walked in with our paint, I saw Aunt Leah sitting on the sofa crying.

"What's wrong, Aunt Leah?" I asked.

"Kit's run away," she said, holding up a wrinkled piece of paper. "She left a note for us saying she's getting married. Do you know anything about this, Ella?"

I didn't know what to say, because I'd made a solemn oath to Kit not to tell.

"What does the note say?" I asked.

She handed it to me, and I read it aloud:

Dear Mama and Pop,
I love you more than anything; you know I do. Except I love Troy Clark and want to marry him. I was afraid to tell you, because you didn't want me going with him. Mama, he is so nice and gentle and you'll love him too. Daddy, Troy can fix anything and make it work. He'll be good to me. I can't tell you where we're going, because you'll try to find me. We'll be back in a few days. Don't worry. We'll be safe.
Your loving daughter,
Kit

I was in a state of shock. She was marrying my own Troy Clark!

"When did they leave?" I asked quietly, trying to bluff my way through this without having to tell a lie.

"She wasn't in her room this morning, so I guess they left after we went to bed last night. Ella, if you know where she might be, you have to tell me. She's just a girl. She's not ready for married life," Aunt Leah said.

"I'm sorry, Aunt Leah," I said, looking down at my shoes. "She didn't tell me she was leaving when I saw her yesterday."

"Now, Ella!" Daddy spoke up, giving me the look. "I can read your face, and I know you know something. We need to find your cousin."

"She told me when we first came back that she wanted to get married, but not who it was. I didn't know they were going last night, Daddy, honest."

The usual gentle Uncle Josh didn't know what to do with himself. He was so mad the veins stuck out in his neck.

"I'm going to find that gal and bring her back if I have to go to Texas!" he shouted and stomped out of the house.

"You and Leah drive the wagon back home, and I'll pick you up," Daddy said. "Troy's got an old rattletrap car that won't go five miles an hour. We can find them by noon, I'll bet."

So off the three of them went, slamming the door behind them. By evening, they were back home, as their trip was fruitless, and Kit was most likely married. All anyone could do was wait.

The next day Daddy and the boys got on with painting the outside of the house white with green shutters. It was good therapy for them. I sat at the sewing machine making curtains out of some pretty flour-sack material, and Nola mainly just pestered me.

"I thought you said you were gonna marry Troy Clark," she goaded.

"That was a long time ago when I was a dumb little kid," I said. "I'm still going to be a singer anyway and won't have time for that old love stuff."

"Anyway, he'll be our cousin now," she said. "And we'll have him around to make music."

"Have who around?" McKinley said, coming into the house covered with green paint from his head to his toes.

"Troy Clark," Nola said. "Did you hear all the fuss about him and Kit getting married?"

"Yeah, I knew they were going to," McKinley said dully and started coughing.

"Did they tell you?" Nola said.

"Troy did. They should be back here tomorrow. They had to go a pretty good ways to find someone to marry them, Kit being so young and all."

That was the most McKinley had talked in days, although he did so with no emotion.

When Dew and Daddy came in, they too had painted themselves.

"Dew, put those brushes in turpentine, and the paint'll come right off," Daddy said. "A couple more days and we'll be done."

That night after Daddy and the boys washed themselves off and ate supper, we all went directly to bed. Tomorrow would be the Armistice Day parade, and McKinley would be in it. I hoped he could show a little more spirit than he did today.

A train passed through town, its whistle screaming, and I wondered if Kit and Troy had seen the same train on their journey back home to face the music.

After the parade the next day, Uncle Josh and Becca met us as we were going to the car.

"They're home, Jim," he said to Daddy. "I don't know whether to count my blessings that Kit's safe or wring that Clark boy's neck."

"I can imagine how you feel," Daddy said. "But there's nothing you can do at this point. You know, I've been thinking ever since this came about that they can live in our old house rent-free as long as they want it. That'll give them a boost to get started."

"I don't know if I can live across the street seeing that scoundrel living with my daughter, Jim," Uncle Josh said. "But back to what I came over here for...Leah wants to make supper for all of us. Can you come to the house?"

Daddy nodded yes, and we all loaded up and headed over to meet the newlyweds. When we got to the house, Kit and Troy were sitting on the sofa holding hands and smiling at each other.

"Well, ain't love grand?" Dewey said teasingly, as he grabbed Becca and swung her around. "Congratulations to you, Troy, and best wishes to you, Kit."

I went over and hugged Kit. To my horror, I started crying, and she started crying, and we were both a mess. It was good that Aunt Leah was in the kitchen rattling pans, or she would have been in on the act.

Nola was sitting off in a corner reading the funnies. She looked up.

"You won't ever get to be a schoolteacher now, Kit, will you? You can't go back to school married," Nola said, raining all over Kit's parade.

I gave her the look, but Kit came to her own rescue.

"I don't want to go back to school. I'm going to help Troy start a business. He's going to sell musical instruments right here in town. He's going to have his band on the side too."

It sounded like they had their lives all mapped out. I went over and hugged Troy, who was sitting uncomfortably, not knowing what to do. The men were all out on the front porch by now.

That's when I heard a wagon drive up. I stared out the window and saw the little boy and the man on crutches coming up the steps.

They were all talking at the same time. I couldn't make out what they were saying.

"Well, gloriosky!" I heard Daddy say in the rumble of words. "What a fine-looking boy!"

"Everyone, come on out here," Daddy yelled. "There's someone I want you to meet!"

The frail man on crutches introduced himself. "I'm Johnny Terrill," he said. "This here's Sonny."

Sonny was either a spoiled brat, or he was really angry about something. He wouldn't speak to us.

"This is our boy—you know, little Daniel!" Daddy said, showing the two into the house.

I was in denial. This couldn't be our baby brother, who had been such a sweet and gentle baby when we saw him last.

But it *was* Daniel, and Mr. Terrill had quite a story to tell.

"I went to the oil fields close to Tulsa. Made real good money. But I had an accident and lost my leg working on an oil rig, so Mrs. Terrill nursed me back to health. Well, a few months ago, Mrs. Terrill got real sick. You know how she always seemed to be imagining her ailments. Didn't think much about it, but the sicker she got, the more I believed her. As it turned out, she had cancer and passed over two weeks ago."

Sonny showed his first sign of emotion. He began sniffling and trying to hold back. I went over to him and knelt down in front of him.

"Do you know I used to feed you milk with a spoon?" I said. "I'm your big sister."

He jerked away and got close to Mr. Terrill.

"Sonny's having a tough time of it. He misses his mother so much. Jim, I guess I need to talk to you at another time. I have some private things to go over with you," Mr. Terrill said.

"Didn't I see you downtown the other day and at the parade today?" I asked.

"Yes, you did. I apologize for acting the way I did, but Sonny's having a hard time getting used to the notion of something I've been talking to him about."

"It seemed like you were mad at me," I said to Sonny.

"I still am," Sonny whispered and looked the other way.

"What did I do?" I asked.

"Just close your mouth, Ella, until we get the entire story out," Daddy said.

"Ella," Mr. Terrill said, "Sonny's not directly mad at you. He's mad at the world right now because his circumstances are changing."

"Time to eat!" Aunt Leah called. Kit was able to untangle herself from Troy long enough to set two extra places at the table for Mr. Terrill and Daniel.

"Sure looks delicious," said Mr. Terrill. "We've been batching it for quite a while now, and I never did know how to cook."

"That's for sure," said Sonny as he looked down at his plate.

We had our feast while Kit and Troy made eyes at each other and held hands. Aunt Leah offered up second helpings at every uncomfortable silence that came up. Uncle Josh was quiet and looked drained of color.

Daddy ate his supper quickly and went out on the porch to smoke his pipe alone. Mr. Terrill followed him out.

"Let's make some music!" Dewey said. "Troy, do you have your guitar?"

"Doesn't everybody keep a guitar in their car to serenade their bride?" He laughed. "Sure, let me go get it out of the turtle."

Dewey picked up Becca, spun her around, and asked her to help him get her Daddy's instruments out.

"I'll help you," McKinley said weakly.

I made Kit go sit down with Aunt Leah in the parlor while Nola and I put the dishes in to soak. At that moment I was in love with myself for being so giving and helpful. But little Miss Nola read my mind and spoke out against me.

"Ella just tries her best to be a show-off. Are you any good at washing dishes, Sonny?" she asked.

"I'm a pretty good dishwasher," he said quietly. "I hate to dry 'em, though."

"Sounds good to me," I said, hiding my anger. "Sonny, what's the story on you?"

"My mama just died, and Daddy's gonna die too," he said in his raspy little-boy voice. "He's trying to give me to you all."

"Why do you think your daddy's gonna die?" Nola asked.

"He said the diabetes is affecting him bad, and he don't have no circulation in his good leg anymore."

"Any circulation, not no circulation," corrected Nola like Miss Rhodie used to do.

"Anyway, Sonny, that doesn't mean your daddy's going to die!" I said.

"Well, that's what the doctor told him," Sonny said.

Sonny was very thorough with his washing and rinsing, and it took us a long time to finish the dishes. Maybe it was good; we made friends, and he didn't seem to be as mad anymore.

The musicians were tuning up as we went into the parlor. I noticed Aunt Leah and Kit had made up and were smiling at each other.

"Get on in here and grab a guitar, Daddy," Dew said. "We're gonna start with 'Old Joe Clark.'"

Aunt Leah sat down at the piano, and to our complete and utter surprise, Daniel sat down beside her, playing right along with her! The jam session began.

Daddy interjected one of his facts about the music they made. He said a lot of it came from the mountain people who had immigrated to America from Scotland.

When they slowed down and started playing hymns, I grabbed Kit's hand to pull her up to sing alto with me singing soprano in harmony. She was asleep sitting up, and it was no wonder after all that had happened in one day!

Luckily, the moon was out bright as day, so we could drive home without headlights. On the way Daddy told us about his talk with Mr. Terrill. The reason Daniel was so mad was that Mr. Terrill had told him we were his true family, not the Terrills.

"Daniel thought we didn't love or want him when we let the Terrills take him. I told Mr. Terrill it might be best if I sit down with the boy and explain that his mama had just died and I was gone more than I was home. There was just no way to take care of him."

Daddy was talking as though he was explaining it to us too.

"Where did he learn to play the piano?" I asked.

His daddy said Mrs. Terrill taught him so he could play hymns with her in church.

"He's pretty good," I said. "Maybe we need a piano for him."

"When do we get Daniel?" McKinley asked in his monotone.

"Probably tomorrow," Daddy said. "Johnny has to go all the way back to Oklahoma and see his doctor there. He told me he is having their piano shipped to us so Daniel can play it."

Daddy turned to McKinley and asked if he was all right.

"I'm okay," he said. "Cough's better."

"He just needs to quit drooping around," Dewey piped in. "He gives me the blues just looking at him."

Before the war McKinley would have punched him. Now, he ignored him and stared straight ahead.

"Just hush up, Dew," said Nola. "McKinley's a grown-up now, and he's not supposed to have fun."

"It'll be nice having little Daniel again," I interrupted, trying to stir up a little peace in the car.

"Yeah," Nola said, "the first thing I'm gonna do is give him a haircut."

"You don't know how to cut hair," Dewey said.

"Do too," she said.

Thankfully, the argument died when we arrived home. Daddy walked up the steps with Nola and me at either side.

"Daddy," Dewey said, "did you ever see Daniel when you went to Oklahoma all those times?"

"I saw him, but he didn't see me," Daddy said quietly. "Mrs. Terrill got so upset every time I contacted them I decided to let the matter rest in peace."

"Didn't you miss him?" Nola asked.

"Just like you did, children. But I knew what was best for him," Daddy said.

"Now, you girls go get some rest and have a good nighty night," he continued.

"Back at cha," we said.

When we got in bed, I lay there for a long time thinking.

I wondered how we kids had even stayed alive all alone while Daddy was away so much of the time. I wondered why we had to be away from Daniel for over five years. I thought about Charlie and the unjustified terror he had endured. I thought about Mama dying so young when she'd wanted to live so badly. Then, I thought about Mack not coming back from the war as the McKinley we once knew.

I asked God to help me make sense of it all and to forgive me for misjudging Mrs. Terrill when I'd thought she was a hypochondriac.

"Also, God, if you have Mama handy, tell her to look down here and see what her baby boy looks like now. He's coming home in the morning."

A train passed, making a peaceful chukka-choom sound just right for rhythm and writing some song lyrics. The thought came to me that Mama was smiling right that minute. Maybe she wouldn't even mind if we started working on Allibeth Bonner to quit teaching school and marry us. Or maybe someday Allibeth and other women teachers could hold jobs and be married at the same time.

But tomorrow our little brother would be at center stage as we tried to help him feel at home in our family. Any schemes to get Daddy back into Miss Bonner's good graces would have to wait. But that was okay. I knew there would be plenty tomorrows to try to right what was wrong with today.

The End

EPILOGUE

Ella never made it to Hollywood or Nashville with her singing ability. She moved to Breckinridge, Texas where she married her one true love whom she met at age eighteen. Her husband was a musician as were her brothers and father and they had a loving, long relationship with music and with each other.

Young Daniel grew up to be a music professor at Vanderbilt University in Nashville where he enjoyed a long professional career. He learned to play every instrument he was introduced to as a child and paid it forward to his own children and others he taught.

Nola married a man whose family owned a clothing store in Little Rock. They had seven children and always kept them dressed in the latest styles. Both Nola and her husband were music lovers.

McKinley formed a country band and traveled the south promoting music from the heart. He married, but had a failed relationship because of his saddened soul following his experience in the war. He was a beloved uncle to all his nieces and nephews, especially Ella's children.

Dewey studied to become a physician with the help of Dr. Jordan and became a leading scientist in the field of medicine. He played the fiddle until his last days and treasured his life in Arkansas as a child.

Katherine and Troy became owners of a musical instrument store in Pine Bluff and lived all their life there. Troy continued to make music with Dewey and McKinley when they all got the chance to be together.

Miss Bonner finally quit teaching school and married Daddy. They had a happy relationship and enjoyed their family and the Arkansas countryside for many years.

Ella and her husband always planned to move to California and grow lemon trees in their backyard while writing and making music. Though they never made it that far west, they kept Daddy and Miss Allibeth on their front burner, hoping they would all move to California together someday. Daddy told Ella they would have to decline because they loved their Arkansas roots. But, they solemnly promised to ride that lonesome train from Pine Bluff twice a year to visit them wherever they might be living.